MURDER AT THE BELMAR

To Linda,
with Best wishes,

MURDER AT THE BELMAR

A tale of Old Mayatlán

A KAY FRANCIS MYSTERY

Looking for Dolores!

B.C. STONE

Bye
BC Stone
23 March 2013

MURDER AT THE BELMAR

Library of Congress Cataloging-in-Publication data

Stone, B.C.
  Murder at the Belmar ; a Kay Francis mystery / B.C. Stone. – 1st ed.

     p. cm.
  Summary : There's malice in Mazatlán, where film star Kay Francis is enjoying a much-deserved vacation, staying at the glamorous Belmar Hotel. Her sabbatical is rudely interrupted when she discovers a dead body in her hotel suite. The deceased lady is mystery writing diva Mavis Wembley, who was visiting Mazatlán to attend an annual reunion of mystery writers, most of whom wish her no good. Cinephile chief of police Capt. Seguro reluctantly accepts Miss Francis's offer of support in ferreting out the many clues and solving the maddeningly complex case. Miss Francis proves to be a more tha capable sleuth, but events progress and there is a desperate race against time to prevent further tragedies from occurring.
  1. Mazatlán (Mexico) – Fiction. 2. Francis, Kay, 1899-1968 – Fiction. 3. Motion picture actors and actresses – Fiction. 4. Detective and mystery stories – Fiction. 5. Belmar Hotel – Fiction. 6. Nineteen thirty-seven, A.D. – Fiction. 7. Nineteen   thirties – Fiction. I. Title.
  PS3569.T6418.M87 2013
  813.54—dc21

"Small things, these, you may think – trifling courtesies that are unimportant in the breathless rush of the world we live in today. Yet our lives are made up of the little things that give us happiness or sorrow. It is only when we lose appreciation of the little things that we begin to die."
- Kay Francis

CHAPTER 1

With some effort the two men dragged the draped body up the stairs.

"It's heavy. Someone's going to see us. What are we doing this for?" Jose Luis didn't bother to hide his impatience and skepticism.

"Don't ask questions," Ricardo said. "Those five hundred pesos in your pocket should be answer enough. And don't worry. Mr. Thrugg knows what he's doing."

"You think you're so smart. Then what about those six months in jail back in Laredo?"

"Shut up! Just do what you're told."

They continued to pull the figure up, up the gloomy stairs toward the penthouse suite where they had been told to take it. The dead weight made a muffled thump with every step upwards. They were using the service stairs but still worried about being detected, and could only hope the lateness of the hour would camouflage their activities and that all the guests in the downstairs rooms were asleep.

The stair hallway was dark and gloomy and the outside quiet, as quiet as it ever gets on Olas Altas Drive during high season. The two men were well chosen for such work – swarthy, rough looking, stocky, dressed in peasant clothes. Their rugged, unshaven faces strained with the clumsiness of their task. They slogged upward with the weight between them as they climbed the blue tiled stairs with effort. They strained the muscles of their strong bodies, but in their fear and desperation didn't feel the strain.

"Just a few more steps, and we'll be there," Jose Luis said.

"Quiet. Someone will hear us. *Dios mio*. Can't we keep the feet off the floor? Check again and make sure you've got the key."

Meanwhile in the suite of rooms upstairs the beautiful woman lay nude beneath the satin sheets of the king-sized bed, contemplating her first day in Mazatlán and reveling in the anonymity and the leisurely pace and the most pleasant surroundings. An added bonus was the ever-helpful Mr. Thrugg downstairs at the bar, who had been so kind to keep her presence undisclosed. She was especially concerned about the writers' group which had practically taken over the hotel, but if any of them actually knew who she was, they too had been respectful of her privacy.

For the first time in a long while she was entirely happy, free from the usual concerns of seeing herself onscreen with the proverbial run in the stocking or a clip not being on straight; her sole worry now was that she might be tardy for tomorrow's breakfast. She sat up in bed, lit a cigarette and pondered. The previous year had not been kind. Her acting skills were undiminished, even improved, but her last two films had flopped and the good roles were no longer forthcoming. Yes, her star was fading fast and soon she would find herself in the death grip of box office poison.

Her looks hadn't diminished since she passed thirty; if anything she was even more striking: the sleepy, pale green eyes set wide apart, large, enticing mouth, dark eyebrows, close-cropped ebony hair, skin that looked ivory in the moonlight, and exotic, slanted eyebrows. With her sleek hair, enigmatic face, compact, lithe figure, and standoffish air, she might well have been one of those prize Siamese cats who tolerate their owners with suave disdain, refusing to be cajoled and won over just because said owners paid a fortune for the privilege of acquiring them.

It all combined to give the impression of a certain worldliness, even a hint of world-weariness, along with experience and sophistication, reinforced by her trademark Deco fashions which she wore with incomparable élan. Like everything else for this brief interlude, however, she was toning down her wardrobe and her striking beauty, instead opting for simple tropical garb and little makeup. Moreover, her dusky looks allowed her to fit in and feel less conspicuous about her celebrity status. Mazatlán was one of her favorite getaways and as usual she had chosen to come alone. Basking in the late afternoon sun's warm glow on Olas Altas beach, savoring the Mexican cuisine and catching up on her reading were a great luxury and tonic for her jangled nerves. The best part was the three more days before she had to get back to Hollywood and the rugged grind of the next project. But for the moment, a much deserved holiday to be savored.

She put out her cigarette and snuggled back into the bed's warm embrace. By now she was barely awake, hovering in that delicious state between awareness and sleep. She felt her body going limp and all sensations vanishing as her head melted into the large, feathery pillow. She faintly heard what she thought was the slightest shuffling of sounds coming from the nearby room, whispered voices, labored, desperate-sounding tones. At first she paid no particular notice, since muffled, shuffling noises in hotels, especially in Mexico, are no great novelty.

She drifted back into her reverie. As always the centuries-old colonial charms of this magical city, nestled beside the Pacific Coast, had worked their special alchemy on her, the smells, sounds, and most of all the light which had lured countless painters, photographers, musicians, and actors. Even for one accustomed to a life of plenty, she felt humbled by the experience and basked in the mystical city's warm glow.

She was drifting again but heard the soft sound of a door closing, then a thud and a groan, then a mumble followed by what sounded like an obscenity in Spanish. There were the sounds of falling books, moving of furniture, and again voices. Too early for the maid. She began to slowly sit up in her bed. Again the voices, two distinct voices which seemed to speak in loud whispers.

In the worst way she wanted to pull the covers over her head and escape all this nonsense in blissful sleep, but the insistent murmurs and shuffles were assuming dimensions too great to be explained away. It was obvious that all the goings on were happening in the suite's adjoining guest bedroom. She slid smoothly out of bed, and the shadows and moonlight sensuously caressed her body in most suggestive fashion, revealing her long and lissom form as she tiptoed carefully toward the master bathroom. There she clasped and put on her light blue satin night gown. Then she began to creep very gingerly toward the next room. Now she was close enough to make out what the voices were saying.

"Can't we speed this up? Someone will find out."

"Relax. Everything's fine. We have to make it look right."

"What's there to make look right?"

Ever so deliberately she opened the door to the next room where she could just make out in the semi-darkness the vague outlines of two forms – two men, and also what looked like a covered figure or perhaps a draped, rolled up carpet on the divan. The two men seemed to be positioning the object, which more and more looked like ...

Impulsively, like the scene in *The Tell-Tale Heart* where the narrator flings open the door and startles his victim with a wild scream, she turned on the light and burst into the room and gave it her all with her loudest and most authoritative:

"Que haces!"

The two men, both recognizable as Mexican laborer types, looked at her, stunned, frozen in shock. Then they screamed and with clumsy movements barreled quickly through the door. She heard their heavy footsteps as they ran through the hallway outside and then down the stairs. She looked around and noticed nothing was taken, and no sign of vandalism. Apparently their only purpose was to place whatever it was they brought in the room, then go. But she had taken them just a little unawares, as it were.

She carefully examined the wrapped up clump on the divan, and as she expected, it was a person, a woman, a dead woman. She looked at her with curiosity. The lady was of a mature age, about seventy years old, and she had an aristocratic air – handsomely dressed, large boned, well coiffured, with a chalky complexion and a prominent, sculpted nose. For a moment she thought she recognized the woman, one of the guests in the hotel perhaps.

"Will you be staying for the night?" She spoke the words in her usual soft, breathy, well modulated voice, but the pungent remark surprised even herself. She looked around to make sure no one had heard her, then continued, "No, I suppose not. It looks like your friends didn't expect me to turn up."

CHAPTER 2

She went back to the main bedroom, lit a cigarette and sat on the bed. Well, so much for the quiet interlude in Mazatlán. But what about the body? Maybe a tasteless practical joke from one of her more zany colleagues from the studio. She knew of a couple of them who would stoop to such lows. Better to check the figure again before it jumped up and started doing a little soft shoe. She went over and drew back the covering carefully to have a closer look at the body. The lady was quite dead.

She noticed thick, clotting blood from the chest and skull. Towels had been placed to quell the bleeding and they were soaked. The lady had been shot at close range, with a small pistol, two gunshots, probably a .22 calibre, which implied the work of an amateur, maybe. But who and why? And why was the killer planting the corpse in her room? She wouldn't put anything past her Hollywood masters for a publicity stunt but this was a little over-the-top even by their standards. No, this was a genuine murder, and the madness had a method. But what method? And why the madness of the planted body? Then again maybe the two ruffians didn't know she was up there; their reaction seemed to confirm this. In any case these two men were just muscle, certainly not acting on their own authority. Whoever was behind this probably knew she was in the suite and thus maybe wanted them to be discovered.

Whatever the explanation, she had to get around to the mechanics of reporting the events. She called the front desk and asked the night man to come up to her room. Promptly he appeared at her door. He was an unassuming little man of middle years, and wore a somewhat smudged white hotel uniform. When he entered the suite he looked at the clump on the divan. As his mouth opened, a dangling cigarette slipped out of the side of his lips. Reluctantly, slowly, he walked over toward the body. He looked at the figure and his eyes widened.

"Dead woman," he said.

"Yes, dead woman."

"Lady regrets *mi Ingles* not so very good. *Poquito.*" He made the universal gesture of the thumb and index finger to designate *poquito*.

With a touch of impatience she replied, "Yes, lady regrets English not so good. *Si, si, entiendo. Es necesario telephonar policia. Comprende?*" She said her words with the speed and confidence of a born actress, moreover, with the authority of one who was accustomed to giving orders and having them followed, but as to her Spanish, her command of the language was no great shakes.

The little man scurried away down to the desk to make the necessary phone call. She waited and lit another cigarette. The morning haze was its atmospheric best and the light was just beginning to filter through the windows, and no longer sleepy, she began to get properly dressed. She opted for a simple white blouse, short pants and lace espadrilles.

Thirty minutes later two men entered the suite. The taller one, obviously more senior in authority, said nothing at first as he wandered slowly through the guest bedroom, then the main room, looking carefully at everything. Then he barked some rapid-fire commands to his assistant, who went into the adjoining room where the body was. Then the senior official addressed her directly. "Captain Seguro, Mazatlán district chief of police, at your service, Madame." He made a cursory bow which hinted of the chivalrous.

Captain Seguro was tall, fortyish, large boned with a slightly bushy mustache, and he wore a simple business suit, not the customary police uniform. Befitting a man of his station, his eyes looked heavy and plaintive, but he radiated a certain bored aplomb which inspired confidence. The small beads of sweat which seeped out of his forehead suggested he made his way to the hotel in some haste. He carefully took out a monogrammed handkerchief from his jacket pocket and gently dabbed the perspiration on his face.

Then he began to light a cigarette, and hesitated as he looked at her more carefully. He slowly drew up his right hand and pointed at her. "I'm sorry to stare, and forgive me for asking, but aren't you – "

A long breath of sigh from her, then, "Yes, I am.

Now what can I do to help you?"

Flustered, he still managed to get out, "Miss Francis, indeed an honor. But please tell me what happened, in your own words." He spoke slowly, carefully, in only slightly accented English.

"Your English is quite good, Captain."

"Oh, thank you. I studied for two years at Berkeley."

She then related to him the night's events, complete with a description of the two men. He told her she'd need to come down to the police station and complete a more formal written report sometime during the day. He went into the adjoining room of the suite and conferred briefly with his colleague, then abruptly came back. "Oh, how remiss. The gentleman in the next room is my executive assistant, Lt. Sanchez."

"Who is the lady?" she said.

"Ah, it's Miss Wembley, the writer. Very sad. She was staying in the large room just below yours, suite 401."

"Mavis Wembley. Yes, I've heard of her."

"Her lawyer and her private secretary are in the rooms to either side of hers. Of course they will have to be notified but we will be generous and let them sleep a little more."

Mavis Wembley. The name was familiar though she'd not read any of her novels. The queen of mystery writers, or something like that. Miss Francis seemed to remember the studio had optioned a couple of her books. Curious, a writer would bring her lawyer to a literary get-together, though more explainable was the secretary's presence.

After a little more conversation the Captain seemed

satisfied with Miss Francis's story and related to her that the two men she described sounded somewhat familiar and assured her he would find them.

She thanked him and took the conversation into unexpected territory.

"This has been such a personal affront; such a clumsy violation of one's privacy and sensibilities, and at such a grand hotel, so unseemly and so tiresome. And as such, and no reflection on you or your colleagues, I feel a certain responsibility to, at least help in the uncovering of who's responsible for this obscenity. With your permission, Captain, I'll do a little looking around on my own, strictly unofficial, to see if I can find more about this monstrous offense."

He took a breath and hesitated, looking straight ahead in a noncommittal manner.

Perhaps feeling the need to convince him, she continued, "I have resources and friends I can call on, and I know a little bit about these writer types. I want to talk to them, some of them anyway, get their stories, see if they know anything, more specifically, to see if they have anything to hide. I want the villain who did this to get what's coming to him."

The Captain was tentative, but accommodating. "*Claro que si*. We would welcome your efforts, in an unofficial capacity, of course. I'm sure you could be … very helpful, in your way, your knowledge and expertise. That business in Berlin last year – "

Smiling at him demurely, she politely interrupted, "But surely you mustn't believe everything you hear about me."

Actually the events to which he referred took place in Bayreuth, but no matter; the compliment was nice to hear but she had mixed feelings about her repute spreading this far. Thus her lackluster response.

She had offered her protests lukewarmly, but the Captain had a diplomatic rejoinder. "Miss Francis is indeed too humble," he said as he handed her a card. "But here's the number at headquarters if you need to talk to me or Lt. Sanchez should you desire any assistance or have questions."

About forty-five minutes later the two gentlemen in the suite were joined by a doctor and another man in a dark grey business suit, a detective perhaps from the police station. After getting Captain Seguro's permission she left the drama in her rooms. It was still early morning and she walked down to the lobby and had a look. The entire downstairs was empty and the restaurant hadn't opened. A cleaning lady was starting to work and looked at her with intense, squinting eyes, then darted away. The night man was at his post at the desk, and Miss Francis smiled at him he smiled back.

The lack of people and movement allowed her to appreciate the hotel's blue tiled inlaid-with-mosaic trim and curving Arabian Nights architecture which gave the suggestion of levitation, a floating Alhambra on the Pacific Coast. As was the case of elegant, large, Spanish inspired buildings, the hotel had a spacious inner courtyard which partially served as an open air lobby which spilt out into the lush tropical gardens. An ornately embroidered, curving ramp of a staircase led to the rooms upstairs.

It was just about six, and she decided to walk, first along Olas Altas Beach. The shore oozed mist and foam and the early rays of the sun began to peek in from the distance. The dawn was arising cool and fresh; everything was clean and graceful, much like Miss Francis herself. Only the thin fog and the faint smell of ocean were old. She took it all in; she hadn't slept and the morning atmosphere refreshed her. But even at this early hour she began to be conscious of the sticky heat which was creeping in and gradually enveloping her skin. She realized some of the lightweight dresses she had brought down with her would be too warm for the climate; she'd have to buy herself some cottons, perhaps some sundresses, too.

She peeled back toward the hotel and turned onto Constitución, walking all the way down to the Plazuela Machado. She ambled along the narrow streets of the colonial center, always happy to be there. She was wearing the obligatory sunglasses which partially obscured her famous features and she discreetly packed a copy of the ever reliable *Terry's Guide to Mexico*, which she carried in her handbag and graced with the occasional surreptitious glance, as she didn't like to give the impression she needed help to find her way around. As she walked she admired the elegant architecture with its remnants of the French influence and, closer to home, overtones of the New Orleans old quarter look.

It was early Sunday morning, hardly anyone around, and she stopped and sat down on one of the little park benches right outside the Angela Peralta Theatre. A suitable place, since she'd heard from the gossip that all the writers here for the conference were at the theatre last night for a gala performance of Maugham's *The Letter*, in Spanish, the Mazatlán premiére, maybe the Mexican premiére, of the famed author's popular play. Indeed, it was rumored the great man would be attending the performance, though she couldn't be certain if this actually did take place. Then a touch of the professional crept into her thoughts: she so hoped the studio would choose her for the role of Mrs. Crosbie – or better still, the exotically sinister Malayan wife – in the upcoming film version. She fancied herself perfect for either character, and she probably was, but then again she always felt this way for the roles she really wanted.

She had a look around and noticed the *Tecolote Café* at the far edge of the plaza was starting to open, a happy occurrence since it was a favorite of hers from prior visits.

She walked over and took a seat, and the waiter Victorio appeared. He was unmistakable in his considerable girth, his round yet sturdy build reinforcing his ebullient mood. His chubby, tanned face beamed at her and he said, "Miss Francis! Welcome back. *Como está?*"

"Oh, *bien, bien.*" She looked at a menu and was pleased to see there was a selection of gringo food to mollify the seasonal Northern tastes. And much as she loved Mexican cuisine she had to be careful with what she ate as to preserve her svelte figure. Accordingly, she ordered toast, papaya, pineapple, coffee and orange juice.

Victorio scribbled the order, went to the kitchen and returned with some coffee and a glass of orange juice. As he poured he said, "Many of your countrymen here last night."

"Truly? Please, tell me about it?"

He seemed pleased to relate the particulars. "Yes.

After the performance. They all stopped here for a late dinner and drinks. They stayed until about one o'clock."

"The writers?"

"Yes, about twelve of them. And the lawyer fellow, Mr. Dumwort, and the lady's secretary too, the quiet one. But the critic, Mr. Delovely, he seemed to be the leader. *Desafortunadamente, la vieja*, Miss Wembley, was not with them. She had taken ill, they said, and needed to stay at hotel."

"Is that so?" She decided not to burden him with the recent, sad news, but rather to let him find out in his own. So Mavis Wembley wasn't with them? Seems convenient she was in her room, a little too convenient. The police said it looked like she was shot between ten and midnight, thus it seemed none of the writer's group could have done it.

She ate breakfast and took in the sounds, sights and smells of early morning Centro. She sat at her table and had a leisurely look around, and liked what she saw. She especially admired the Casa Machado which overlooked the square from the West end. The gracious old estate and private home was a veritable time capsule of the best of Old Mazatlán. The Plazuela Machado was named after a nineteenth century magnate and industrialist, and the square was the oldest and most beautiful in town, with proud old buildings, mostly private homes, which gave it a friendly Old World feel.

One version says this Machado fellow built the block-long plaza, topped off by a gazebo stage which projected itself proudly, surrounded by tall lilting palms. It all conjured up the romantic feeling of a vaguely

Italianate European town square. Another version of the story puts the Casa Machado first and the rest of the plaza buildings as dating from the 1880s, when Machado himself was long gone. In any case it was a spectacular collection of French, Spanish and Italian style buildings right here in the New World.

She thought about what she'd learned so far, trying to make some sense of the details. All the writers had been at the performance, and then later they gathered at the nearby *Tecolote* for drinks and some carousing until about one o'clock. As much as the usual motives of envy, revenge, greed, whatever, would be second nature to such pride-driven individuals as writers and would-be writers, circumstances suggested none of them could have been the perpetrator of the terrible crime.

But if not one of them, who? Alas, the murderer simply must have been someone else, but who was he, and, more important, why? A husband, or business partner? Her lawyer was here in town, a curious situation for a writer's conference. He was as good a first choice as any; lawyers are natural born suspects. He would have to be looked at a little more closely.

She finished up her breakfast and wasn't quite ready to go back to the hotel. Instead she felt strangely invigorated and wanted to walk. She started in the direction of the lighthouse, said to be the highest in the world. Up, up she strode with her usual focus and confidence, negotiating the high curving terraced walkway that circled to the top of the mountain and led up five hundred-odd feet to the top.

Her strong legs and lean condition made the walk more bearable but it was still a bit of a challenge and a good leg stretcher, and as such helped to take her mind off the recent events in which she found herself – admittedly by her own doing – now enmeshed.

Even at the relatively early morning hour she felt the heat and, more so, the humidity, as it clung to her skin and clothes and wrapped her in its sweaty embrace like some large predatory animal that had hold of her and would not let go. On the positive side, she was wearing good shoes and light clothing and had the foresight to bring along some water. And some paving and stairs made the climb a little easier. The hill upon which the lighthouse was perched was known as Cerro Creston, or Creston Hill, located at the south end of Mazatlán with spectacular views all the way up. She stopped a couple of times along the way, more to admire the wonders of the scenic vistas than from fatigue.

Finally she got to the top. Her legs were shaky and she was hot and sweaty but the accomplishment felt great. From this high promontory she could appreciate the city's San Francisco-like contours: green hills, white houses clinging to them like encrusted barnacles, the bay and ocean backdrop.

Mazatlán was tucked away on a thin finger of a peninsula curving into the Pacific, a huge arc of curves that ranged all the way from the rocky southern cliffs of the peninsula to the palm-laden northern beaches. She saw down below the waves breaking against the golden-brown rocks along Olas Altas Beach. Even more stunning was the entire greater city of Mazatlan which lay below: the cruise ship and ferry docks, Old Town and its cathedral, the restaurants and entertainment of the Playa Olas Altas and the various beaches to the north along Playa Norte and Puerto Viejo Bay. She couldn't hold back the feeling that it was all hers, for the moment anyway; she had taken on El Faro and had bested it.

After descending the hill she walked back to the hotel. It was still Sunday morning, albeit late morning. She recognized the man at the front desk who greeted her. He was the day man, Carlos, a very affable fellow with a good command of English. He said, "The authorities have designated your room a crime scene and you have been moved to Room 422, a very nice large room, ocean view. We took the liberty of gathering your things."

She affected a mild sigh, more of boredom and fatigue than anything else. "Oh I suppose that'll be all right," she said nonchalantly. But more serious, she realized her impulsive volunteering had a few consequences, principal among them being she would need some expert assistance. It was time to call on the services of one Johnny Caballero, a B actor who occasionally dabbled as a private detective and had done various jobs for her in the past.

"Telegram please," she said to the attendant. The clerk gave her the necessary form and she wrote on it rapidly.

Johnny Caballero, Hollywood Calif. Johnny your presence urgently needed. Please come to Hotel Belmar in Mazatlán. I've got work for you. Important. Kay.

She handed the message to the clerk and told him to get it out as soon as possible. She then had a light lunch at the hotel restaurant, and with nothing much else to do she retired to her new room. She turned on the ceiling fan, read for a bit and settled in for a much welcome nap, as she was in need of the sleep she was denied last night.

She woke up in late afternoon and knew it was time to talk to Mr. Thrugg, the master bartender and a good source of local gossip. He would probably be at his post by now. She walked through the lobby toward the bar and noticed several writerly types present, sitting quietly and looking forlorn. Also two men who didn't fit. They seemed to be lurking, hovering, waiting for something to happen. She pegged them as reporters, and wishing not to be noticed, quickly sneaked into the bar and took a seat in a nearby booth. Tucked away and with dark lighting, the bar made for a good place to hide. Only a few scattered customers were present. The ceiling was lower and the room smaller than one would have expected. The large window's Venetian blinds faced the walkway on Olas Altas Street. There was a piano in the far corner, and a dapper pianist was playing a flowery rendition of *La Paloma*. The dim lighting and claustrophobic atmosphere gave the bar a more than usual sense of the seedy and conspiratorial.

She got up and walked toward the bar, and Mr. Thrugg smiled broadly in his usual gregarious manner.

"Ow goes it, Miss Francis?" He spoke with a thick East End accent, and his smile revealed quintessentially English teeth – crooked, pointed, not especially well cared for. She'd heard he was a bit of a rogue, and he looked the part. His tanned face was sweaty and had a pockmarked, fungoid quality, his features something of a synthesis of Wallace Beery and Lon Chaney. He could have passed for a retired rugby player, and for all she knew he was one. What little she did know of him was sketchy: a journeymen who had found his way to

Mexico. A perfect fit for his new job as he could converse in English, what passed for English anyway, with the hotel's mostly American clientele.

"Oh, *bien, bien*, thanks," she said.

"Can I fix ya' a drink?"

"No thanks, I'll just have a Coke."

"Coke it is." He poured the Coke into a small glass and filled it with ice. As he brought it back to her he said, "A bit o' the drama in your room last night, I hear."

"Quite, but not so much as in Miss Wembley's room."

"I reckon yer right. Her friends over there seem a bit down at the mouth." A nod back into the hotel lobby.

"Yes, but no sign of the lawyer, Mr. Tumworth."

A self satisfied smile, then, "Now there's one with somethin' to hide. But we all have somethin' to hide, all exceptin' myself, of course."

"Au contraire, Mr. Thrugg; you seem the type who has a lot to hide."

They stared at each other for one awkward moment. He hesitated, mouth slightly open, just enough for her to notice; for such a breezy individual who always had a ready comeback it was a bit out of character. But he recovered quickly.

"Oh now, Miss Francis, surely you mustn't talk tha' way. It may not be … how do they say, profitable."

She felt a shiver on her back; he really seemed to mean it. This time she was the one who recovered.

"Speaking of things to hide, you were saying something about Mr. Tumworth?"

Mr. Thrugg returned to jovial mode. "Right you

are; word 'as it he was gettin' the sack from Miss Wembley after this little outing."

"Fired? If this was the case, why even bring him here?"

"Search me."

She cocked her head and said, "How do you know this?"

"She tol' me."

"Miss Wembley?" Miss Francis didn't hide her incredulousness.

"Nobody but."

"Have the police talked to you about this?"

"I was just gettin' to that part myself … no, not a bloomin' one of them, but we've got to remember this is Mexico and they doing things a little different like down 'ere. Anyway, I guess they 'ave their own suspects but it would be a bit of all right if they'd at least give a poor old sod like myself some hint of recognition with a little suspicion. Me, I'm kind of sensitive 'bout these things, you know."

Was Mr. Henry Thrugg joking or was he genuinely miffed at being overlooked? Well, in any case he was just the hotel's hired help, and as such had no direct connection to the deceased lady. All the same he seemed the sort who basked in the notoriety. She thought a change was in order.

"What do you think about the secretary?"

"Ah, Miss Niffin. Sweet thing. Mousy, retirin' type. Not seen much of 'er. She's cloistered herself in the room, beside herself with grief. I suppose she'll have to talk to the authorities eventually, they're roundin' em up pretty thorough for official statements and all. Anyhow, word on the street was she and the missus was a little more than just yer usual type friends, employer and employee, and then some, if you get my meanin'."

"Yes, I think I do."

She gradually wrapped up the conversation, politely thanking him for the insights. Then she wandered back over to the lobby. From his comments she got the impression that Miss Niffin – and Mr. Thrugg himself – were persons of more than passing interest, in particular the congenial yet strangely unsettling Mr. Thrugg. For all his garrulousness there was something about him she found disturbing and uncomfortable, right on the edge of downright evil. But all this was neither here nor there, for the time being anyway. These were just feelings and impressions; what she needed was facts. With this in mind she prepared for her next interview, but without much enthusiasm.

Miss Catherine Wentworth and Jack Favell squirmed in their seats in the too small lobby sofa. They were a couple, and insisted on doing this strictly unofficial interview together, but, as Miss Francis already surmised, were none too happy about it, especially Miss Wentworth, whose auburn hair was a trifle mussed. This, along with the plain business suit which she wore, signaled a subtle sign of disrespect in Miss Francis's direction.

"What kind of a police operation is this, using self-appointed amateurs to talk to us instead of the real authorities," huffed Miss Wentworth.

"Quiet my dear, here she comes, she might hear you."

"Then let her hear me. Good lord, what an insult.

It's flattering to be considered as a suspect, however in passing, but why do we have to be subjected to this washed up film queen turned amateur sleuth"

Favell clasped her hand and put a benevolent palm of his other hand on her shoulder. "Dear Cathy, always so impetuous, aren't we? She has the confidence of the local police chief, you know," he said with a reassuring lilt to his voice.

"Of course she does. What do you expect? He's nothing but a smitten fan. Probably has designs on her; she has quite a rep that way."

"Hush, here she is."

Miss Francis sat down on the sofa across from them and said, "Well, can we begin by saying this is awkward for me as well. But I believe I can be of help to the local authorities in the process, and quite surprising, they believe so too."

"If you say so," Miss Wentworth retorted tartly.

"You must forgive Cathy; she speaks her mind," said Favell, trying to play the apologetic diplomatist.

"Yes, well, right. Well, could we begin by asking what is your connection to the deceased Miss Wembley?

"We're her long lost illegitimate children?" Miss Wentworth delivered her words with an affected rectitude which was mixed with undisguised petulance. "Good God, what do you think, you silly woman. We're fellow writers, obviously." She was now veritably snarling the words.

"Cathy, please, your indulgence, Miss Francis is doing the best she can in this difficult situation." He turned in Miss Francis's direction. "You must forgive Cathy; she's under quite a strain. We're exactly what she said, fellow authors, but not quite as successful or accomplished as Miss Wembley. We'd hoped to pick up a few tips while here. Actually my primary line is screenwriting; I've a couple of B movies to my credit." He primped his hair and seemed pleased to sneak in a reference to his current occupation.

"Oh, really." She was happy for the subtle change of direction and wanted to continue so. "Could you to describe your activities last night?"

Miss Wentworth glowered and said, "We've been all through this already with the local police, such as it is, we've even filed our own written reports."

"Yes, but there's always the possibility of something new being discovered, isn't there?" She tried to be a business-like and neutral as possible. "Speaking of which, what were your last recollections of the unfortunate Miss Wembley."

Miss Wentworth blurted, "This is impossible. Jack, I just can't do this anymore."

Jack Favell clasped her hand gently. "Cathy, your indulgence. Just a few more moments." Then he turned in Miss Francis's direction. "Well, to your question, we saw her here in the lobby having drinks, talking with colleagues. She seemed to be in good spirits. As far as we could tell she was planning to go to the performance at the theatre. Then she talked to a couple of people and walked to the desk, spoke to the night man then walked toward her room. I noticed her movements were a little unsteady as she was walking."

"What about the secretary?"

"We saw her at the play, sitting up in fourth balcony. During interval she was talking to a platinum blonde who looked a little like Jean Harlow. They seemed to be having quite an animated conversation, but in a friendly sort of way."

After a few more innocuous questions and answers, she curtly wrapped up the audience with Miss Wentworth and Mr. Favell, thanking them for being so generous with their time and such.

She felt a sense of relief at being finished with the difficult couple, especially the snippety Miss Wentworth. By now she was getting tired and needed to clear her head, so she went outside and started to walk, down one of her favorite streets, Angel Flores, of the famous elevated sloping houses and the tilted sidewalk and wall, which had lured many painters and photographers, most notably Tina Modotti and Edward Weston.

She walked all the way down to the main part of town and stopped in the cathedral by the plaza to collect her thoughts. She was not a religious person but the noble atmosphere and grand architecture helped to soothe her somewhat frazzled nerves. She wondered: did she really need this? Was life as a movie star so bad? After all, she was under no obligation to do anything. Was it just a fool's errand, a tribute to her own vanity? She had to admit to herself she liked Captain Seguro's compliments about her positive repute. But she shrugged off such thoughts as she left the cathedral and walked to the mercado, the main covered market in town, built by the same fellow who designed the Eiffel Tower and one of the biggest covered markets in all Latin America.

Happily it was Sunday and quiet, not the usual cornucopia of sounds and colors and movements. She stopped at a little cantina call *Pepe's* and had a taco suave and a Coke for a makeshift dinner. She then strolled down to the little plaza at Zaragoza and sat and listened to a band concert performed by school musicians, a welcome respite. She then read for a bit, a novel, James M. Cain's *Serenade*. The time went by fast; it was now eight o'clock. Where did the afternoon and early evening go, she wondered as she began to walk back to the hotel, but this time in the somewhat out of the way route by way of Icebox Hill along Olas Altas St., which gradually curved back round the hill, hugging the shore line.

She stopped beside a high bluff on the walk and in the distance along the shore to the North she noticed a crowd of watchers forming on the walk and at the shore. The men in boats rowed slowly toward the beach and the men in the bay walked backward, tugging a net as they came, until they were knee-deep in the waters. Then the small vessels gradually edged toward the shore, and the crowd grabbed the net, dragging it on to the beach. She could see the huge net sparkling with fish, and she heard the voices of the fishermen and their families. The net was open and women caught live fish by their tails and carried them away from the crowd. Tiny sardines fell out of the nets and rolled across the sand. The sunlight reflected off them and they looked like tiny strands of silver. Miss Francis mentally noted that the folk had been fishing that way for hundreds, even thousands of years and she merely nodded approvingly then continued her meandering.

She walked past one of her favorite spots, Cerro Vigía, about a quarter mile south of Olas Altas Beach. It was was for hundreds of years the lookout point for soldiers watching for pirates and marauders on the horizon. Also in the evening twilight she glimpsed the Cerro Creston, which she had so triumphantly traversed earlier that morning, its stump of a mountain rising spectacularly in the distance and housing the lighthouse, the soothing beacon of light of which had long been a great landmark to ships far out at sea.

Feeling a little exhausted, she strolled back into the lobby of the *Belmar* and just then to her great surprise she noticed Johnny Caballero lounging in one of the cozy rocking chairs. She walked directly toward him and he began to stand up. "Johnny! How did you get here so fast?"

"Connections, dear Kay, connections."

"Well, however you managed it, you're a welcome sight. I've a job for you."

CHAPTER 3

An uneven night's sleep. Simply too many sensations, sounds, smells and images from the day to take in. At one point she dreamed she was in Oaxaca during a wild Carnaval celebration, an orgy of colors, masks, costumes, popping balloons and firecrackers everywhere. Funny, because she'd never been to Oaxaca. She awoke in a sweat in early morning, around four a.m. She smoked a couple of cigarettes and pondered the events so far. Johnny's presence reassured her; he was a capable fellow and probably on the job already. Another nice development, too: all the writers and various hangers-on had been told they couldn't leave the city, for the moment anyway. Ever the lawyer, Mr. Tumworth had made a few harrumphs and mumbled something about contacting the American consulate, but even he was cooperating. She dozed a little more, and finally arose, got dressed and went downstairs to the little outdoor café adjacent to the hotel lobby. It was still early in the day, and only few customers were present: a writerly looking couple she didn't recognize and, inevitably, it would seem, Miss Wentworth and Mr. Favell. Being in no mood for trouble, she took a table far away from them.

Feeling a little bruised from all the effort, she allowed herself an indulgent sampling of rich and tasty foods: rolls, buns, *pan dulce* and cake, along with jam, honey and a small bowl of cold fruit, all washed down with some strong Espresso. After all, one meal wouldn't ruin her world class figure. Johnny C then showed up at her table as pre-arranged. He wore a white shirt and matching white slacks and shoes, and sported a thin mustache which accentuated his wiry, dapper frame.

"Well, John, what have you got?"

"Not so much, Miss Francis."

"Please … I always go by Kay."

"'All right … Kay. Well, I found out through the grapevine that all the parties of interest were at the play, then at the restaurant afterward, so it looks like none of them could have done the deed."

A thoughtful nod. "So it would seem. What else?"

"Well, there's also talk down at police headquarters about an American woman, some kind of actress they think, whose body was found, over in a place called the Juarez district, something of a rough part of town. Looks like it was murder. Anyway, word has it she was here for the play and took a wrong turn. No apparent connection to the Wembley case but I though you'd want to know."

"What's going on in our quiet little town? Murders happening all over the place." She paused in thought, then said, "But it's odd … Captain Seguro didn't say anything about this when I spoke to him just a few hours ago; he must want me to find out about it in the papers; probably afraid I'll poke my nose into this case as well."

"Could be."

"I'm sure that's it; I don't think he's any too happy about my snooping around the Wembley murder but he's putting a good face on it, Mexican politeness and all that. But, Johnny, check into this one a little more; see what you can find out. Who knows, maybe we've got this all wrong, limiting our suspects to just the writers here for the conference. It's possible there's another explanation; maybe the two are connected in some way, a Jack the Ripper-type madman, perhaps, or someone who's got it in for the gringos, something like that."

"Will do."

"Anything else?"

"Well, the scuttlebutt is that Captain Seguro and his men are closing in on those two thugs who transported the body to your room."

"That's a good development, but it can only get us so far. Anyway, I have a new task for you. Later this morning I'll be interviewing the lady's personal secretary, Miss Niffin. While I'm doing so I want you to go up to her room – I know you're good at getting into rooms – anyhow, look around for anything … juicy. A diary, perhaps, receipts, documents, letters. Whatever you find bring them down here and signal me. Then I'll pawn her off on one of Captain Seguro's men."

"Got it."

Miss Francis was conscious of the hotel lobby's not so comfy sofas as she sat directly across from Miss Niffin and tried to figure out what to make of the loyal secretary. Dressed in shades of grey, brown and browner, the girl stood out as the poor relation in such a stylish crowd. This was further reinforced by her plump physique, which she seemed to be self-conscious about. She nursed her glass of wine; unlike the other guests, drinking alcohol didn't seem to come naturally to her.

Miss Francis began to speak, leaning forward as though she was imploring the girl. "You've known, oh, sorry, – you knew Miss Wembley for some time."

"Yes." She had a slight cold which accounted for the punctuations of sneezes and sniffling, all the more obscuring her tiny voice that was almost a whisper. She wore a dowdy, rounded wide brim hat which awkwardly covered much of her face, which was hardly necessary given she was usually looking down or away.

"You and Miss Wembley met a few years ago?"

"Yes, back East. She hired me as a private secretary about ten years ago when she began to get busy. Soon after we moved to California." The girl spoke with an affected upper class accent but there were also touches of Midwestern twang interspersed in her conversation.

As Miss Niffin spoke Miss Francis tried without success to gauge her demeanor and response to the questions, but had difficulty getting a good look at her with all Miss Niffin's diverted glances. Must be the poor girl's pathological shyness, she thought, compounded by the recent events. Probably in a state of shock, poor thing. Accordingly, Miss Francis did her best to expedite things.

"Then you were with Miss Wembley for about ten years?"

"Yes. Ten wonderful years. Such a great woman, very talented, and such a joy to work with." Miss Niffin coughed and sniffled about every two or three words and it further obscured what she was saying. It all made for a frustrating interview, yet Miss Francis was game and made one more attempt.

"Can you think of anyone who would want to do her harm, for any reason?"

The girl's wisp of a voice was now practically quivering. "Honestly I just can't think of anyone; she was loved by everybody. Even the critics adored her, and her fans, you know, were, well, just legionary, and thought she walked on water."

That everyone loved her was debatable, but what did one expect from a loyal, admiring employee? Miss Francis sensed she wasn't going to get a whole lot out of the grieving Miss Niffin and needed to wrap things up.

"How did she get along with her colleagues? The folks here, for example."

"Oh, very much; they all admired her so, even more than her fans I would say. You know, they looked to her for inspiration, and she was so generous with them."

They talked for another five minutes, mostly on the events of the past couple of days, and Miss Niffin's account provided no surprises. After they wrapped up the formalities of the interview, Miss Francis arranged for Miss Niffin to go with Captain Seguro's man to the police station where she would fill out a formal written report. Miss Francis could see Johnny gesturing in the wings near the kitchen. She went over to him and he smiled broadly.

"This!" he said triumphantly as he handed her a small book. "A diary, no less."

"Pure gold, Johnny boy."

"And these."

He clasped in his hand some writing papers which looked like handwritten drafts for a play or novel. At the top of a page was written *The Thief Who Came to Dinner*. She read a few passages. The style had an elegant touch and showed true writing talent. Was she emulating her mistress? But even more revealing was the diary. An entry dated two days ago began:

Again in Mazatlán where the goddess rides on the waves and the souls are born … is there a more scenic setting in the world … the wonderfully twisty, turny streets with the Francophile buildings with a touch of the Florentine about them, Mazatlán, where anything can happen, magic and mischief lurk behind every corner, the Byzantine structure of the old city seems to invite intrigue, even inspire one to pen crime novels… the spirit sings upon return and the poet weaves its spell and times runs backwards at a languorous pace … and yet, is there any mystery left in me *… do I possess a* me, *or is it the circumspect nature of things that has brought me to this state?*

She read some more, and it went on in like fashion, a combination of perceptive eloquence and flowery, pretentious excess. She returned the materials to Johnny and told him to take them back to the room and put them back exactly as he had found them. But it was curious; were these diary entries and scraps of creative fiction the musings of an amateur under the spell of the great woman who was her mentor as well as employer? Or perhaps it meant something else. Whatever, there was a lot beneath Miss Niffin's placid, self-effacing surface, which rather reminded her she'd neglected to ask Miss Niffin directly if there was anything ... unusual in her relationship with the her employer. Right or wrong, to her own satisfaction Miss Francis had concluded there was not. Nonetheless, there was something a little off-kilter, strange and disturbing about the secretary, and especially her writings. But what was it, and what did it mean?

CHAPTER 4

Even on holiday in Mexico, Harrison Tumworth had arranged his hotel room in a manner which bespoke of a faux-British grandeur. He insisted on having his conversation with Miss Francis in his suite of rooms on the fourth floor, and he seemed to have brought half his Beverly Hills office with him. There was a *Southern California Legal Directory*, *California Legal Handbook* and of course the Martindale Hubbell volumes, all ten of them. These and various other legal tomes, notebooks and ephemera proudly projected themselves from the makeshift bookcases which crowded the edges of the suite's adjacent second room, which he had transformed into a legal sanctum sanctorum. Moreover, the scattered photos, certificates and other memorabilia which were prominently displayed veritably screamed history and tradition.

He'd also added a little furniture of his own,

probably to the hotel management's combination of horror and delight. His touches were mostly Tudor Revival, a heavy, vintage carved oak. Drapes, too, of a burnished gold. A large oak desk dominated the center of the room. To the left of it was the obligatory bar stocked with all manner of liquors. Perched conspicuously on his desk was a bottle of Evan Williams which seemed a little incongruous but somehow just right. On the floor were thick large throw rugs of a deep brown which obscured the exquisite Talavera tiling which sparkled throughout the hotel. But the quality and tradition of the hotel tile couldn't have mattered a whit to Tumworth. He wanted his suite to impress, and as such its present, changed decor filled the bill and matched its tenant perfectly. It all immediately placed the scales of power in Tumworth's favor, which was probably the norm for him.

The imperious Tumworth was, among other things, lawyer to the stars and sophisticate extraordinaire, but most of all a classic British gentleman of the old school. He spoke in a deliberate, viscously Oxbridge style and pronounced his words with a ripe plumminess. He also liked the ladies and was said to be a man of not inconsiderable charm when it suited him, especially when arguing a case. In any event he looked like a cross between a college professor and an Anglican bishop, and though he wasn't particularly old, he put on a good act of being wise, benign and endearingly befuddled. You couldn't imagine Tumworth ever screaming or raising his voice, except perhaps for theatrical effect for an enraptured jury.

His portly body looked well fed and his round, California-tanned face projected the sturdy self-assurance of one who clearly belonged to the elite class, and knew it. His brown eyes were focused and intelligent, and he had the semi-charming look of a man who didn't smile so much as he hinted he was just about to smile, which gave him an affable uncertainty and served to camouflage his razor sharp mind.

In view of the tropical climate he was absurdly dressed in a dark brown pinstriped suit, matching tie and Florsheim dress shoes, with gold watch and chain proudly displayed.

Miss Francis wanted to pour chilled water over him to wake him up, or better yet, plant a passionate kiss on his lips – unpalatable as such a thought might be – just to see if he was alive. This was the modern era, 1937 after all, but Tumworth reeked of a Dickensonian aroma, half fragrance, half malodorousness, all overlaid with a whiff of British arrogance, and his suite cum office was everything Miss Francis loathed and loved about England. As she walked into his room he looked up at her. Affecting a vaguely dithering manner, he shuffled some papers on his desk, but they were little more than stage decoration.

Finally he said, "Ah, yes, Miss Francis. I wish I could say it's a pleasure, but let's suffice with a how are you?" The words rolled off his tongue like pearls on cushiony velvet.

"Oh, *bien, bien*."

"Please, let's keep it in English, shall we?"

"As you wish," she responded curtly. With such a character Miss Francis knew she would have to tread lightly and as such chose her words carefully. She had to be delicate for other reasons; it always stung Tumworth that Miss Francis employed other legal counsel, not his, and she knew of his feelings.

"Now what can I do for you?" An unnecessary question, as he already was very much aware of her, however unlikely, role.

"Let us be clear, Mr. Tumworth," she began, "I'm just assisting Captain Seguro, with his full approval, and my job is simply to collect evidence and information, and thus I'm not to be thought of as a formal interviewer grilling subjects." She emphasized the last few words in mock threatening fashion.

"My dear Miss Francis, well, yes, I would certainly hope so. The whole arrangement strikes me as highly irregular, to say the least, but since this is Mexico, and a different set of rules apply, I'll try not to stand on ceremony and make too much of a fuss of it."

"I appreciate your understanding and cooperation."

"Not at all. And in any case this type of unorthodox approach sometimes yields good results, a fresh perspective and all that."

She smiled and seemed pleased with his near compliment. "Very good. Then may I begin at the beginning? You're quite well known in the film industry as lawyer for a number of major stars." A mild nod of acknowledgment from Tumworth. "You were also the deceased lady's personal attorney?"

"Ah, quite. Her attorney for business matters as well. In both cases for nearly ten years. After she became a major success she knew she'd need some top-notch legal advice."

The unspoken question which hovered in her mind like a purple elephant dancing in the room was Mr. Thrugg's comment that Tumworth was about to get the sack from Miss Wembley. But she thought better of expressing her curiosity directly. Rather, she proceeded carefully, but not too carefully. "You accompanied her to Mazatlán on what might seem was little more than a glorified vacation. That's a bit odd, isn't it?"

"Yes, I'll admit it seems a bit unorthodox, but in my case I considered it a working vacation. I visit Mexico from time to time and Miss Wembley had some legitimate work for me to do when I was here. And much as I enjoy the holiday aspects of being here, for me work must come first. It's why what you see here in my hotel suite resembles something like a law library."

His last comments caught her off guard. She didn't know about his being here in a working capacity. But she continued in stride. "Really? Well, I'd like to come back to that, but first may we proceed to some of the recent events here?"

Tumworth responded with a matter-of-fact and noncommittal, "By all means."

Miss Francis adjusted her position in the chair. As luck would have it, the chair was not one of Tumworth's imports, and as was the norm for Mexican furniture the level of elegance and workmanship did not translate into comfort.

"May I begin by asking some background on this writer's group, things like who they are, when they meet and the like?"

Tumworth affected an oily, rather self-satisfied smile accompanied by an assured nod. "The writer's group, indeed." He got out a cigarette holder as he spoke, then inserted a Players cigarette and took a first puff, all done with theatrical effect perfected over time. Then he poured himself a half glass of bourbon. "Cigarette? Or a little something to brace you for your detective tasks?"

She demurred to both.

"As you wish." He put the glass to his lips. "Chin-chin," he said, as he made the gesture of a toast and took a small swig. "A little early in the day, but there you are."

She didn't figure a fellow of Tumworth's calibre needed a drink to steady his nerves when dealing with an amateur like herself. Maybe it was just another of his lawyerly tricks to throw her off.

He took a long breath and continued, "They call themselves the Southern California Mystery Writers' Circle. They formed about ten years ago. By the way I'm legal counsel to the group collectively as well, but only to Miss Wembley individually. They fancy themselves legitimate mystery writers but really Miss Wembley was the only one of any professional stature or success. Miss Luckingham a little bit; it was well known she was the heiress apparent to the throne. Anyway the rest of the lot are mediocre talents and self-styled hangers-on, all hoping a little of Mavis's magic would rub off on them."

"And Mr. Doveless, the critic?"

A smile and mild horse-chuckle, then he said, "Percy Doveless, theatre and literary critic extraordinaire, or so he would tell you. No, he has no literary ambitions as such, just likes hobnobbing with the writer types, and I think he likes the tropical atmosphere, in all its, shall we say, mysterious ways." He delivered the last phrase with an inquisitive raised eyebrow. "But he's worth looking at a little more closely, that one. Maybe he has one or two things to be … discreet about." He let the last sentence hang there like a piece of candy in front of a child, hoping she would pounce on it.

But she proceeded, "Anything more you can tell me about the writers' group?"

A small breath of impatience, then he smiled, lifted his glass in a small toast and took another sip of his drink. "Well, they meet once a year, usually here. There's no real substance to their meetings; despite the high-toned title, it's really more of a social club than a professional society. Basically they like getting together, having a good gossip, comparing notes, that sort of thing. This year was a little different; they were going to present Mavis with some kind of lifetime achievement award, which would consist of a nice plaque and a special surprise, a one of a kind, specially printed, leather bound edition of her first novel, *The Vicar Takes a Holiday*, that they all had signed and were going to present to her at a gala dinner. Very sad." He shook his head pensively as he said the words.

"Yes. Quite. But who on earth could have had a motive to kill her in such brutal fashion, then transport the body upstairs to my suite?"

"Yes, that must have been quite a shock for you. As for motive, means, opportunity and all that, I just don't see the members of this group as being very good suspects. They aren't the nicest people in the world, mind you, some of them anyway, and despite the aforementioned efforts on her behalf, not all held Miss Wembley in great affection. But I don't see any of them as the murdering type, and I've got a little bit of experience in these matters."

He sat upright, a look of triumph radiating from him, as though he'd completed a brilliant chess move. "So, Miss Francis, you'll have to look elsewhere, I'm afraid. But I dare say we have plenty of candidates right here in Mazatlán, even amongst the guests at the Belmar. All those Hollywood types and oil barons. How does Mr. Maugham put it when describing Monte Carlo, a sunny place for shady people. He could well be referring our picturesque little town here."

"Perhaps so. But continuing along the line of possible suspects, what was your impression of the secretary?"

Another oily smile. "Quite the little mouse, isn't she? No, I don't think you'll find much there. She's practically invisible; no one knows much about her, very low profile. This was the first time she'd made the trip with Miss Wembley."

"How about Mr. Thrugg down at the bar? He seems quite the ruffian."

"Right you are, and you may have something there, the ruffian part anyway. But again, what's his connection to Miss Wembley? And what's the motive?"

Miss Francis seemed a bit distracted; Tumworth did have a point. She looked out the window, then her concentration returned.

"But to get right to the nitty gritty, Mr. Tumworth, and believe me, I am sorry I must ask, but could you describe your movements two days ago in the evening and later into the night."

Another cultivated, unctuous smile. "Very much so. And by the way, please call me Harrison. When you address me as Mr. Tumworth it makes me feel a hundred years old," he said in a mock conspiratorial tone with just a hint of a wink. "Anyway, I had a few drinks with the writers in the bar, from about six till seven thirty, then ambled over to the theatre, marvelous production, even if my comprehension of Spanish is a little limited. Anyhow, then I went with the others to the little café, and came back to the hotel around one o'clock and went to bed. And, no, I didn't see or hear anything untoward. I'm afraid I was feeling a little tipsy from the tequila and fell asleep right away."

"Did any of the behavior of the others strike you as out of the ordinary?"

A breath, then a leisurely, "No … they seemed to be themselves. Kind of leaves you in a quandary, Miss Francis. These are without doubt your most likely suspects, and it appears none of them could have done it."

"Perhaps not. But you said something about your being here in some sort of official capacity?"

"Ah, yes, I thought you'd never come back to that. Among other things I was tidying up a few legalistic details as regards the new book. But probably of greater interest to you is the fact that Miss Wembley brought me down here to change her will. I was beginning to draft just such a change when the tragic events occurred. No reason to keep it secret, since it was never finalized. Anyway it would all come out in the official investigation. And since I'm sure you're wondering, the substance of the new, never finalized will was that, after a few charitable contributions and a token amount for some distant relatives, she left the bulk of her estate to her faithful companion and secretary, Miss Niffin."

"Really?"

"Quite. And now there's no new will and everything reverts back to the old will, which is much more along conventional lines, in which the secretary gets a modest stipend for her good work and the money gets spread around, in, some would say, more just fashion."

Miss Francis tapped her pencil on her pad and nodded slowly. "It would seem to leave out motivation for Miss Niffin, since the new will was very much in her favor."

"Not necessarily. As far as I know, Miss Niffin didn't know anything about the contents of the new will. You see, Miss Wembley played her legal cards pretty close to the vest."

Mis Francis nodded. "And I don't wish to tread too indelicately, but there's some gossip Miss Niffin and Miss Wembley shared a relationship that was a little … how does one say, unconventional."

Tunworth didn't seem at all surprised at the indiscreet question. "Yes, I've heard those rumors, too. You see, Miss Wembley never married, and accordingly such gossip would seem inevitable. She and I never really discussed her private life but from what I observed she liked the men and loved the fawning attention she got from them. So in my my viewpoint, no, I saw nothing unnatural in her relationship with Miss Niffin."

A bit bored with this line, Miss Francis wanted to change the subject. "I understand she was just finishing up her new book."

"Yes, that's was my understanding as well," Tumworth said, feigning some interest. "She was putting some final finishing touches on the manuscript here. It was called *The Long Lavender Goodbye*. A different kind of book for her, it treaded into areas a respectable mystery writer isn't supposed to write about, or so I'm told. But you see, I wasn't involved in the aesthetic aspects of her publishing career, only the purely legal."

"Once again, I must ask about the secretary and her possible involvement in preparing the manuscript."

"No, no, her job was strictly for more prosaic matters, you know, correspondence, paying the few odd bills, that sort of thing. Miss Wembley was a stickler for typing her own material."

"Is the manuscript here?"

"No, probably not. The bulk of it, maybe all of it, should be at her publisher's office, Far West Publishing in Los Angeles. The best person to talk with would be Mr. Randall Lane, the editor and publisher; he can fill you in on the details. From what I hear it was due to come out in a couple of months. And they were going to give it the full marketing treatment, you know, using words like *daring, sizzling* and the like."

For a man who didn't get involved in artistic matters, Tumworth seemed pretty well-informed. Miss Francis scribbled some more notes, then fussed a little more with her position in the uncomfortable chair. But she regained her focus.

"Is it possible her new book and its 'sizzling' contents has some connection to the recent, sad events?"

"I suppose anything's possible, but I think it unlikely. She's done this kind of thing before, thinly veiled caricatures, real events presented as fiction, just more subtly."

"I see."

"I'm glad you do." Another smile, half ingratiating, half condescending.

She gradually wrapped up her encounter with Mr. Harrison Tumworth, thanking him profusely as she bid her farewell. He'd given her plenty to mull over but alas relatively little of substance she could tie to her investigation. As to his own supposedly imminent dismissal, she just didn't see it. Maybe Tumworth was a great actor – that was part of his professional repertoire after all – but Miss Francis didn't get the impression he was on the outs with the great lady. If so, why bring him here as the crown jewel in her entourage and set him up in such regal surroundings? No, Tumworth may have been worthy of suspicion – his whole manner was a combination of evasive and just a little too smooth – but the notion he was about to be sacked and this constituted motivation for murder just didn't convince. Besides which, he had lots of other high priced clients in his pocket. And there was the little detail which couldn't be overlooked – he had the perfect alibi.

Then what prompted Mr. Henry Thrugg to make such a comment? Idle gossip? Or just a flight of fancy? Or did he have a more sinister purpose, trying to muddy the waters for his own agenda, but what might that agenda be? As for the new novel, and its supposedly sensationalist contents, there might be something there, but was it enough to kill over?

It was almost noon, and she was beginning to tire of the interviews, her fatigue augmented by the frustration she felt from her lack of progress. She went down to the little hotel restaurant and had a light lunch, then retired to her room, where she wrote a sentence or two in her diary, then read for a bit and settled in for a long nap. When she awoke a few minutes before five she noticed an envelope which had been slid under the door. It was stationary of the highest quality. She opened it and

immediately recognized the elegant, Edwardian-style
handwriting and unmistakable trademark Moorish
symbol embossed on the paper at the top of the page.

My Dear Kay,

*Please forgive me for not contacting you sooner, as all this
social whirl has kept me so terribly busy. I'm staying at the
governor's mansion up on the hill near the school; they practically
insisted. Reluctantly I accommodated them though I'd much
preferred to have lodged where you are. The Belmar sounds like my
kind of place, and my kind of people. Anyway, I've been cajoled
into attending some sort of art opening between five and seven at
the* Dos Tertugas *gallery over on Niños Heroes St., and if you
could stop by for a gossip that would be marvelous.*

Your faithful servant, WSM.

She beamed widely and could hardly contain her
delight; a diversion like this was most welcome,
especially so with such distinguished company.
Although she would barely have time to get to the
event, she insisted on adorning herself properly; no
wardrobe restraint this time. She hurriedly dressed
herself in a form fitting, off-white, full length silk
Vionnet dress with bright red satin belt – she looked
great in reddish tones, and knew it – and open toe black
suède shoes, all topped off by a pink cape and one of
her famous, rounded peekaboo hats. And despite her
usual disdain for jewelry – diamonds were cold and
hypocritical, rubies garish, and pearls egotistical – she
decorated herself top to bottom with the finest stones: a
gold brooch, long pearl necklace, emerald earrings,
ruby bracelets, and two sapphire rings on both little
fingers.

Her clothes seem to melt down her shoulders and

creep languorously over the rest of her five-feet nine inch frame, flowing like warm honey over her full, sylph-like body; her attire, along with the jewels, provided just the touch of soigné that toned down and partially obscured her almost too obvious sensuality.

As she strolled toward her destination she noticed a few heads turned to look at her. Though this was nothing new in her experience, she enjoyed the attention. She proceeded and found the *Dos Tertugas* with no problem. It was a large converted private home, almost an estate, and as was the case with the grander residences from the old days, had a generous, well lit patio with lots of the tropical vegetation, tall palms, luxuriant flowers and the sound of the occasional exotic bird squawking.

The guests were the expected well-heeled crowd, along with, curiously, a sprinkling of radical looking types and self-styled intellectuals. Champagne flowed and there was lots of food everywhere. The pleasant, dull purring of string quartet music emanated from some obscure source. It sounded like Mozart to her, or was it Haydn? She could never quite tell the difference. Then she saw, towards the back of the gallery, what appeared to be the guests of honor, two persons, an unlikely and somewhat peculiar looking couple. They looked vaguely familiar but she couldn't quite place them. The man was tall and beefy, six feet five and at least two hundred fifty pounds, with a puffy face and a generous paunch. He wore rumply, worker's clothes and had on some kind of peasant hat. He was surrounded by four admiring, well dressed ladies who were listening intently to his every proclamation. The woman at his side, his wife presumably, was small and petite, maybe five feet two. She was dressed very elegantly in bright, colorful quasi-native clothes. Her black hair was worn pulled back and it seemed to be stuffed with all sorts of fruits and flowers.

Just at this time she heard a strong voice. "Kay darling!"

She looked to her left and there he was. "Willie, so good to see you, a great pleasure as always."

He smiled broadly, clasped her hands and planted a firm but discreet kiss on her cheek. "So good you could come. My boat leaves tonight, I'm afraid, for Asia – these long tours will be the death of me yet – but better to see a little bit of you than not at all."

Somerset Maugham was the very picture of the dapper sophisticate, impeccably groomed in white dinner jacket, red carnation, black tie, dark slacks and shoes. In his right hand he held the ever present cigarette holder. He wasn't an attractive man, and the years had not been kind to him, but he carried himself with such éclat and vigor that all found him little short of irresistible.

"I heard you were in town," she said, "but I didn't know if it was just a rumor."

"Well, you see, I'm really here. By the way I loved you in *Another Dawn.* Of course I'm not exactly unbiased since the film was based on one of my stories."

"Very much so, and many thanks for the compliment. But I'm afraid the critics and audiences weren't so generous."

"That's when you've got to fight them," he said, making a fist and delivering a mock punch downward into the air.

"Perhaps you're right. But getting back to tonight,

isn't this an unlikely venue for you?"

"Not at all, my dear, this isn't just *any* artistic couple. It's Diego Rivera, the great Mexican muralist, and his wife, Frida Kahlo, a pretty good artist herself. Good people, a fascinating couple actually, even if my politics is a little at odds with Señor Rivera's."

She shook her head in a slow, knowing up and down motion and said pensively, "So that's who they are. I knew they looked familiar."

"Maybe later I can wangle you an audience with them, but they seem pretty occupied now. The ladies just adore Rivera, and he positively revels in the attention. Which is all the better. I wanted to talk to you about your new role as resident sleuth."

"Oh, you heard about that?"

A sigh from Maugham. "Like so many places, Mazatlán's a small town really and news gets around. Anyhow, I wanted to talk to you about Miss Wembley and her unfortunate demise. I expected her at the performance. She was a guest in my booth; we're quite good friends, of course. Well, about fifteen minutes before the play was to begin, this note was delivered to me, from someone who said she was Miss Wembley's secretary. The whole thing struck me as highly irregular, and I wanted you to have the note. It may assist you in your investigations."

He gave her the small piece of paper and she read it, but was not convinced there was anything amiss with it.

My dear Somerset, I seem to have taken ill and will not be able to attend The Letter. *I'll see you tomorrow perhaps. Love and kisses, Mavis.*

"What about it seemed irregular?" she said.

A rather haughty jerking back of the head from Mr. Maugham. "Well, first of all, she never addressed me as 'Somerset', nobody has for fifty years, if anybody ever did. My good friends and colleagues call me 'Willie.' Second, she never signed anything with 'love and kisses'. But most important I know her handwriting and this isn't it." As he said the words he pointed emphatically toward the note.

"She could have dictated it to her secretary."

"True, but the whole thing has a bad odor to it if you ask my opinion. But happily for me that's your job. Which reminds me I'd better go over and flatter Mr. Rivera and Miss Kahlo, all the while trying to keep Trotsky's name out of the conversation. Will you join me?"

"No, I don't think so; the company's fascinating, but I feel a little out of place."

"As you wish."

She gave him a big hug and kiss. "*Bon voyage*, my dear Willie, a great trip to Asia."

She strolled the premises and had a cursory look at the paintings displayed. They were all so bright and modern; she never could warm to this kind of art. She left the reception, happily before someone else had recognized her. Before she knew it she was walking along Olas Altas Drive. It was one of those wonderful early evenings, a little after moonrise, when the sky was deep indigo and a few twinkling stars showed through and the full moon was hanging over the Pacific.

It was a treat to see Somerset Maugham again; it had been two years, during her last visit to London. She was tempted to do a little lobbying for the role of the female lead in the upcoming film version of *The Letter*. But it might be a little unseemly, since she didn't want to take advantage of their personal friendship, preferring to get the role on her own merits. She was always a stickler for that. She wandered back to the hotel and indulged in a few thoughts, such as who was this Diego Rivera and his wife. And what was their connection to the political exile Leon Trotsky, of all people.

She went to her room for a few minutes, then walked down to the bar for a pre-arranged appointment with Johnny Caballero. She noticed Mr. Thrugg wasn't working, rather there was an understudy at his post. Then she saw Johnny, who looked dapper wearing a light grey guayabera shirt and matching slacks and shoes without socks. He was puffing on a thin Cuban cigar and nursing a glass of Johnny Walker as he sat in one of the bar's large cushiony chairs.

He got up to greet her, beaming as she walked up to him. "Kay, you look simply smashing."

"You look pretty rakish yourself. Anyway, I read about that dead women in the papers but your message said you have a little more."

"I do. To begin, it seems the woman was one Leah Lavish, from Santa Monica."

"Leah Lavish? What kind of a name is that? Sounds like a fan dancer."

"You're not too far wrong. Papers they found on her, an her actors guild card, driver's license, union card, confirm she acted part-time and worked various other odd jobs: waitress, cleaning lady, that sort of thing. But the folks down at the theatre say she wasn't a cast member for *The Letter*. Her murder happened on or about the same day of the Miss Wembley murder. The police report said her face had been – " He hesitated.

"It's all right; I get the message. Not much to go on, is it? It sounds like the police kept the important stuff to themselves. Good digging, Johnny. Now what of the motive?"

"They didn't find any cash on her. Theft?"

"Maybe. In any case I never heard of her; Universal isn't my studio. As for why she was here, that's not so unusual; lots of film stars like to drop down to Mazatlán, but they tend to be major stars, not an up and comer like our Miss Lavish."

Johnny pressed the connection angle. "But we've got the two murders so close together, both Americans here on holiday."

"Yes, curious, isn't it? But on the other hand, Miss Wembley and this Miss Lavish were of different ages, professions and social classes. Moreover, these murders were committed in different parts of town, so perhaps the two crimes have less in common than meets the eye and we're looking in the wrong direction."

"As usual, Kay, you're way ahead of me."

"Well, maybe. Anyway, I've got more work for you; use your contacts, whoever, to leave town tonight."

Johnny's face brightened and he smiled.

She reached into her handbag and withdrew two regular size business envelopes, which she in turn handed to him. "Johnny, I want you to take this first envelope to the main entrance to Warner Brothers and show it to them. If there's any trouble have them contact me here immediately."

He glanced over the contents of the note in the envelope. It was written in her usual elegant hand, with the unmistakable vertical, not overly angular lettering, the capitals stripped down to just the size necessary.

Mr. Johnny Cabellero is carrying an urgent dispatch for me, to be delivered personally to Mr. Errol Flynn. Below is my signature and seal, both of which you are familiar. If there are any questions please contact me at Hotel Belmar, Mazatlán. Kay Francis.

"And here is the letter to be delivered personally to Mr. Flynn." She handed him the envelope. It was addressed *Mr. Errol Flynn Esq., Warner Bros Studio, Personal and Confidential.* The envelope was sealed. Johnny wasn't going to get to see the contents but only be the messenger, which stung a little bit, but he accepted his role stoically. "Another thing for you to do, Johnny: I want you to poke around Far West Publishing, discreetly, mind you, and find out what you can about Mavis Wembley's new novel *The Long Lavender Goodbye.*"

He smiled in his most mischievous manner; he relished the opportunity to use his more specialized talents instead of being employed as a mere errand boy, and this did much to restore his self-esteem. And he said as much. "A chance for my lock picking skills to be exercised again."

Miss Francis frowned and shook her head in a disapproving manner. "Don't tell me how you're going to do it, just do it."

"Understood. By the way, what's with that title, *Long Lavender Goodbye*? Doesn't sound like a mystery to me."

"Forget about the title; just find out what's *inside* the book. Read it, all of it preferably, then get back to me.

Also, find everything you can about Mavis Wembley, her background, her first novel, when she moved to L. A., things like that. Now off with you!"

No sooner had Johnny left she remembered her appointment with the redoubtable Percy Doveless, theatre and book critic for the *L. A. Journal*. Percy had asked her to meet him at *Rosalinda's*, an outdoor bar and café on Olas Altas Drive at the other end of the street just a ways up the hill, in the general direction of the lighthouse. It was rumored the food there was among the best in town. She barely had time to get upstairs and change her attire, but otherwise was happy to oblige him.

She approached the restaurant and noticed, per usual, Percy had chosen the most conspicuous table available, right by the front entrance on the outdoor deck. She saw him wrapping up a chummy conversation with a delicate, fey looking Mexican man of about twenty years. The young man slithered away and Percy arose from his seat and planted a delicate kiss flush on her lips.

"Kay dearest, you look just divine. How is it you never seem to age?"

"Percy, you're such a love," she said, in mock coquettish fashion.

Percy's compliment was nice, but a little misplaced, as she was dressed in canvas shoes, white ducks and a man's polo shirt. But for her shapely figure underneath and shock of luxuriant black locks, she looked more like a ship's mate than the glamorous woman she was. Moreover, she was feeling a bit tired and frazzled and knew she didn't look anything near her best. She didn't know him very well but since he didn't review movies she'd never been the victim of his brittle wit, and for that she was grateful, and it made this audience easier.

Like so many of the writers here for the conference, he was decidedly overdressed, wearing a cream colored suit and Arrow shirt, white neck tie and white loafers, with red rose tucked in his jacket lapel. Percy Doveless wasn't exactly good looking but he projected himself well and had a certain *je ne sais quoi* which might best be described as an ethereal presence more often associated with the demure romantic heroines he critiqued in his writings.

He wore his light suit as though it were his second skin, and his vaguely Near Eastern labyrinth of a face, topped by the questioning, raised eyebrows that rested on his preciously wrinkled forehead, hinted of a taste for exotic temptations. One got the impression of a male undine of delicately perfumed sensuousness and sensibilities, and as such, decidedly a creature of pleasure. All the more surprising then that his countenance usually bore an expression of half bemusement and half seriousness. This was reinforced by the thick, dark rimmed glasses which he wore, which gave him the flair of an intellectual.

He immediately took out his pack of cigarettes and lit one with a graceful fluidity that made it a mini-pantomime. He offered her one, which she refused.

She continued with pleasantries for a bit then got right to it. The subject of the new book inevitably came up, and Percy warmed to the conversation. "Dearie, if you think anything she might have written in the book would offend *me*, think again. I'd have been flattered to make an appearance, thinly disguised, as they say. And anyway in these circles my proclivities are well known." He pronounced his words with a nasal lilt that hinted of the snobbish and the precious.

"Yet Mr. Tumworth seemed to think there was some sort of racy material there."

Percy's face frowned as he huffed, "That rumpled old windbag. Just likes to hear himself talk, thinks all those monologues he gives before captive audiences in court gives him the liberty to make literary pronouncements. What would he know of the contents of Miss Wembley's next novel?"

She nodded in semi-agreement.

Percy calmed himself and continued, "Anyway, what made this novel different wasn't anything salacious in the contents; she was experimenting with new ways of structuring her writing in terms of plot, form, stream-of-consciousness, that sort of thing. She was tired of cranking out the same old story again and again. She wanted to try some of the things writers like Joyce, Hemingway, Fitzgerald were doing, incorporate them into her work. An art novel disguised as a mystery, if you like. Sure the publisher wanted to promote it to the hilt and would advertise accordingly – remember, the sizzle always sells better than the steak – you should know that from your profession."

"Perhaps you're right, Percy. But the frustrating thing is … can anybody tell us about Miss Wembley herself, who she was, what she liked, her intimate friendships, romantic interests. So few people seem to know anything about her; everyone wants to talk around her, but not about her."

"Well, I can tell you she loved the fame and

financial reward of being a great mystery writer. But as for everything else, nobody really knew her. She was a very private person. Oh, she played the role well, did the public face and all that, gave interviews and book talks, came across as vaguely eccentric and absent-minded in the best British tradition. Yes, she was a good public persona for the books but as far as anyone knowing anything about her … " He raised his hands open palmed in a gesture of frustration.

Miss Francis took a slightly different course. "Indeed, but if I could change the subject a bit, what was your connection to the writers' group?"

A self-satisfied smile from Percy. "Of course. I was what you might call an ex-officio member. I suppose they saw my presence as adding a little glamour and credibility to the proceedings, a certain critical imprimatur. My being an admirer of Miss Wembley's work and the good reviews didn't hurt either. I'd like to maybe do a little creative scribbling of my own some day after I shed this critic's skin, and I hoped that by hanging around I'd pick up a few tips, by osmosis, if you will. And I just plain like Mexico. There are certain freedoms, residual benefits, of a holiday here. One doesn't have to tip-toe around, look over one's shoulder and be so careful."

As she listened to Percy talk she sneaked in a few glances inside to the main area of the restaurant. The customers were mostly American tourists, also a table of better-class Mexicans, plus a sailor or two on shore leave. The musicians were playing and a girl was dancing, not the phony Spanish dance-style you could see in the floor show of a Los Angeles night club with a Latin name. It was earthier, livelier but also more innocent. The dancer wore Oaxaca-style garb which was made up to look like flowers: a large flounce of starched white lace on her skirt and another such around her face. When Miss Francis looked closer she could see the headpiece was nothing more than the skirt of a child's dress, with the hem draped around the face and the rest draping down the back of the dancer. The young woman was lost in her dancing, and the crowd clapped with delight.

Percy took another sip on his brandy, then a leisurely puff on his cigarette, and waved to a table of young Mexican men in the far corner of the restaurant as he continued, "But speaking of being careful, I suggest you look more closely at Miss Luckingham."

"Why would that be?" Miss Francis had heard what the others said about her but wanted Percy's version as well.

"Well, as you probably heard, after Miss Wembley, she was the only one of this motley collection that had any real talent, and it was common knowledge she was tired of endlessly being the queen-of-mystery-writers-in-waiting, and maybe wanted to speed up the process."

"You think she would resort to murder?"

He shrugged. "People have murdered for less, I suppose. I wouldn't put anything past her; she's very ambitious, you know. And there was the bit the other night where she and Miss Wembley were overheard arguing, fairly energetically, at the little restaurant next door to the hotel. Miss Luckingham threw her wine glass on the floor and said something to the effect she wasn't going to wait indefinitely and she wouldn't stand for this any more. That's fairly dramatic … and fairly suspicious."

"Well, I would say so. Certainly I'll pursue this."

Funny. No one had mentioned that little incident to her. If it was true it elevated Miss Luckingham to the status of top suspect. And if Percy's other, admittedly self-serving comments proved to be accurate, then he was off the hook. It seemed then the new novel didn't have anything in it that someone would go to such extreme measures to exact revenge. But as for the final verdict on that, she awaited Johnny Caballero's opinion when he looked over the manuscript. She got back to the conversation and asked a few more questions. There were no revelations, and ultimately he talked her into joining him for a light dinner, and indeed the meal was excellent.

CHAPTER 5

Captain Seguro had requested her presence at the station, so after finishing her breakfast at the hotel she dutifully went to police headquarters, remembering to bring along a small paper bag which contained a wine glass which she had suggested his men have a look at. When she got there she was ushered with much deference into his small office in the back.

He smiled broadly as he greeted her, clasping her hand and giving it a discreet kiss. In view of his rank his work area was unassuming and spartan, a simple cluttered desk and the usual police citations and certificates lining the wall. What caught her eye was a picture of what was certainly the wife and children perched on his desk. Also a signed photo of Dolores del Rio on the wall amongst the other police memorabilia. She had to wonder whether he really had business to discuss or did he just liked having her around. Maybe a little bit of both.

"You're a film buff?" she said, gesturing with a nod of her head in the direction of the photo.

Slightly flustered, Captain Seguro managed a "*Poco.*" His protest was half-hearted but, pleased with the cinema reference, he seized the opening. "But permit me if I may, and you'll pardon the informality, I've seen all, well, most of your films. I love them all but my favorite is *Trouble in Paradise*, a most wonderful film, very popular in Mexico, and no disrespect to your co-star Miss Hopkins, I think you and Mr. Marshall were the better couple and it should have been a better finish to the story if you and he had ended up together. But how you say in English? What do I know?"

Miss Francis mused that Captain Seguro was not only a movie fan but something of a romantic, but she kept her thoughts to herself. "Not at all, Captain, your comments reveal you're quite sophisticated on your movies."

He smiled and breathed a sigh of relief.

Then she continued, "As to your idea of the film's ending, I suppose a lot of people felt as you do, but for me the film's denouement was perfect in its way, a touch of the bittersweet, to be sure. Yes, Madame Colet was one of my favorite roles, too. Such a pity tastes today don't allow the same kind of spice and suggestiveness in the dialog. How the world changes in a few years."

She looked away pensively, then said, "But if you'll allow me to get back to the business at hand."

"By all means." His answer was the spirit of accommodation but his long-faced demeanor suggested disappointment that her mini-lecture on film history was over.

"This," she said proudly as she handed him the bag which contained the glass. "Your men can do their worst."

"*Por supuesto que si*. I suspect this will yield some interesting revelations." He went out into the main area of the station and handed the bag to one of his assistants, then returned to the office. His manner had a dignity and courtesy, of which there was nothing ingratiating, and what he communicated next convinced her he had some real substance this time. "I requested you come in here to ask on your progress and to tell you of two, rather significant developments."

"That sounds most encouraging," she said. "Could you tell me of the news?"

"But first, if I might request, your findings."

"With much pleasure. Alas, I don't have a lot at this point. Everybody points the finger at someone else. Mr. Tumworth seems secure and has a perfect alibi. Well, they all do, for that matter. He says Mr. Doveless has much to hide, but when I talked to Mr. Doveless he claims he doesn't mind his peccadillos being known. And he says it's Miss Luckingham, Miss Wembley's chief rival, who's the real villain, and that I should be looking at her. Meanwhile, Mr. Thrugg says there's something not quite right with Mr. Tumworth, and it goes on and on. But, happily, I've two good sources I've called on who are digging a little deeper, and soon things will begin to clarify."

"That is reassuring. But as to the official developments, the two ruffians who moved the body up the stairs to your suite have been found, up in Concordia, a small town about thirty miles North, in a gambling den, squandering their money. No doubt they thought they were far away and thus safe from the reach of the police. Never a good plan, in our country or yours."

"Very good, Captain, my congratulations."

The Captain nodded, then continued, "Their names are Jose Luis Gonzales and Ricardo Muñez, both well known to us, petty criminals, smugglers, thieves. Sometimes they even do legitimate work as fishermen. In any case no doubt they thought they had gotten away, how you say, scot-free. Both had the same story, which they were happy to tell after the inducement of a possible reduced charge. And I'm inclined to believe their story is true. But there is a little problem."

"What problem is that?"

"They both said Mr. Thrugg from the hotel bar paid them five hundred pesos each, some real money in our country, to move the body upstairs, *como se dice*, no questions asked. An unorthodox request, illegal, to be sure, but not the worst of all possible crimes. I can see why they were tempted."

"Sounds plausible. For all his affability, our Mr. Thrugg had culpability written all over him. But I don't see the problem you spoke of."

"Yes, indeed. I would very much agree with your opinion of this character. Most unsavory. The problem is, Mr. Thrugg has simply disappeared."

"Yes, I noticed he wasn't at his post at the bar the last couple of days."

"Good perception on your part. At this point we can't determine whether there has been foul play or if he simply fled because of his own reasons, of which there are probably many, quite aside from this body moving business."

Miss Francis looked away thoughtfully, then said, "But of course the question is: what does it mean? Was Mr. Thrugg the murderer and did he want to frame me? Or frame the two petty criminals? Or perhaps he was merely the go-between for the actual murderer, and what was his connection with the murderer?"

"Many questions, Miss Francis. I have the same questions, and until we produce this Mr. Thrugg, or whatever his name is – our investigations suggest this is an alias – I'm afraid our knowledge of the facts is limited." He took a puff on his cigarillo and walked across the room and picked up some papers. "But, on the other hand, in certain, other areas we have a little more evidence to work with." He handed her the papers. They were some kind of police forms on regulation size paper with single-spaced text on them.

"These are the transcripts of the interviews of the writers, as well as the secretary and Mr. Tumworth. All done in English, translated and transcribed, truly a challenge, I assure you. They have been looked at and signed by each individual as representing accurately their oral statements. What I would like to request of you is that you examine them and see if you find anything … unusual, or of interest."

"With much pleasure; I'd be very much interested."

"Then I'll leave you to your documents. Please, anything you like. Coffee, soda, whatever, my man is right outside."

"No, thanks, I'll be fine."

He left the office and shut the door. She took out a cigarette, lit it, took a first puff and then looked over the written reports. Alas, they pretty much jibed with what she had heard already, all of it in some detail. They all agreed they last saw Mavis Wembley at the bar at about seven o'clock, that she retired and went to her room, they all went to the theatre, then the restaurant, and so on. But a couple of the transcripts stood out, for different reasons. The first was Miss Luckingham's, she of whom Mr. Doveless had found so suspicious. The operant section of her transcript that caught her eye was:

A couple of nights ago Mavis and I decided we'd have a little fun with everyone. We always found it amusing that I was designated as her heiress apparent. Anyway, we liked to have our practical jokes at the expense of the others and we thought a little mock argument between us, right out in the open, would be just the thing. It was at the little restaurant next door where some of the writers were dining. I thought I was at my theatrical best, shouting a few indignant phrases and stalking away in a huff, even smashing my wine glass. As I'm sure some witnesses will mention this as certain proof of my guilt I just wanted to clear up the matter before it gets taken to larger proportions than it deserves.

So Claire Luckingham wasn't denying the incident had occurred. Clever of her – the true touch of a mystery writer – to get her suspicious act right out in the open so it could wither on the vine. The pre-emptive strike, as it were. Maybe she'd been coached by Mr. Tumworth; it sounded like one of his lawyerly tricks. But this was an unlikely explanation, and in any case a rather uncharitable thought on her part. But the real question lingered: was Claire Luckingham's version true, or just a clever subterfuge? It was time to have a talk with Miss Luckingham.

Also interesting was the account by the secretary. Not really the content, even in view of the curious business of the note of regret to Mr. Maugham. No, it was something else, something about the tone, but at this point Miss Francis couldn't quite put her finger on it. She re-read one of the paragraphs.

Miss Wembley asked me to take the note to Mr. Maugham. I did so. He seemed disappointed. I took my place in the theater up high in the fourth balcony. I do not like to sit close to the writers. Most of them were down in the main area near the stage. After the play I went with the writers to the restaurant. We had dinner and some drinks. They did most of the talking. I went back to my room around twelve thirty. I went to sleep and didn't see anything.

Curious she didn't say anything about the mystery woman with the platinum blonde hair that Mr. Favell had gone out of his way to speak of. But that was neither here nor there. In fact it was only Mr. Favell's story. At any rate it wasn't just the specific facts Miss Niffin related, it was something else in her account that Miss Francis found unsettling, but she wasn't quite sure what it was.

Ninety minutes later she had finally finished reading the transcriptions. She was rather tired, and a little hungry, and her mind was beginning to drift as Captain Seguro entered the office, his countenance revealing a delicate sense of urgency with the serious expression on his face and his slightly distracted demeanor.

"Your indulgence, Miss Francis. But we have an interesting, somewhat colorful, and recent development, of which your especial knowledge might shed some light."

"Whats that?" Her tone was more skeptical than quizzical.

"If you would most kindly follow me."

"Yes, of course."

He led her down a gloomy corridor, the walls of which needed scrubbing in a most desperate way, and they arrived at their destination, an interrogation room. He knocked and they proceeded inside, into a shabby room which consisted of a table, small file cabinet and three chairs. The smell of stale tobacco hovered over the room, and inside sat a uniformed officer in the corner, keeping watch on a somewhat dandified man who was seated at the interrogation table. The man was in his mid fifties and had a thin, rakish mustache. His hair was medium length and slicked back, and he had a perfect nose and profile which tended to accent his slightly furrowed forehead. He was fastidiously dressed in a brown, Prince of Wales three-piece suit with wing collar and tie. His eyes danced with alertness as he said, "Ah, Captain, my dear friend, a glorious day, is it not?"

The Captain responded matter-of-factly, "Yes, indeed, a very nice day."

The man looked at both of them, but turned his attentions quickly toward Miss Francis as he examined her carefully and with obvious admiration, looking up and down her elegantly statuesque figure. "And who is this, may I ask? She reminds me of Navarre. Or should it be Navarrette? Navarrita perhaps? No, to be more precise, a creature of most delicate beauty. Or better yet, that thing that – the something that just pours out of a lighthouse lamp, a light, a glow that bathes the psyche and will not let go. How does the poet say it, if she didn't already exist she would have to be invented, the rare being whose reason for living is beauty itself." He spoke with the intensity and focus of one on the fine edge of madness, though not quite there.

Looking a bit impatient, Captain Seguro gently interceded, "Yes, quite so, but if we could get to the business at hand."

"Yes indeed, by all means, my good man." He articulated his rather rapid speech with a well modulated exactness, his words flowing like smooth gin sliding down the back of one's throat. Each nuance of posture matched his speaking, and carefully tendered movements punctuated his body language. His perfectly groomed fingers smoothly stroked a pair of white gloves, then the hands crept over to the brim of his sporty fedora which he held. The lines of his mouth bent to a subtle intimacy, then slithered to a smoothly menacing grin. But Miss Francis intuited that his malevolence, veiled behind his rather glassy eyes, was benign. She instinctively recognized in his persona the unmistakable touch of the theatrical, and by inference, the fraudulent.

Captain Seguro dutifully contributed, "To begin, this is Miss Francis. She's assisting us in the investigation."

A shy smile from the man. He got up from his chair and clasped her hand gently, then gave the hand a delicate kiss. "*Enchanté*, my dear." Miss Francis merely took a step back and nodded in response.

Captain Seguro continued, "Would you please relate to her what you told us just a while ago?"

"But of course, my good man, but of course. The gist of it is: I killed Miss Wembley."

"What!" As she exclaimed the word Miss Francis's head jerked in the direction of the man.

"My young lady, certainly your hearing does not fail you. But to indulge you once more, I killed the great authoress." Then an inquisitive turn of his head and raised right eyebrow. "But who *are* you, my dear lady?"

"Never mind who *I* am, who the devil are you?"

He glanced in the Captain's direction. "Your colleague did not tell you? Oh, very well," he said with a long sigh as he slumped back into his chair rather nonchalantly. But he pulled himself up and his ramrod-upright posture returned as he said, "I am Ignatius T. Portifoy, villain-in-chief and crime genius, but first and foremost nemesis to Miss Wembley's eponymous hero Mr. Clive Baxter. Here's my identification." He reached into his jacket's inner pocket and took out a wallet, opened it, retrieved a card and gave it to her.

"I never heard of you," she said as she took the card from him, looked at it perfunctorily then gave it back to him.

He leaned backwards stiffly in his chair, his manner affecting an indignant, taken aback pose. "You've never heard of me? Then, my dear young lady, you must get to know your Mavis Wembley better." He turned in Captain Seguro's direction. "My dear Captain, are you sure you've got the right investigator on the job? She seems woefully uninformed even in the most basics of Wembley scholarship."

"I'm sure Miss Francis is the right person for the job," the Captain answered.

Miss Francis continued her train of thought, "The thing of it is, Mr. Pointneroy, or whatever your name is, or rather, the question is *not* whether I'm the right person for the job, but whether you are … just who the devil are you, what are you doing here and most important – if it's not too much trouble – would you mind recollecting just for our convenience, how you did the deed to which you confess?"

Another indignant stiffening of the body. "Never mind how I did it; that's my little secret. It's your job as detectives – I speak to the both of you collectively – to figure it out. But I warn you – my method was most ingenious."

A deep, rapid sigh and sideways shake of the head from Miss Francis. "This isn't going to get us anywhere. Let's get out of here."

A nod from Captain Seguro and they both left the room.

They proceeded to just outside the police building. Captain Seguro addressed her in most contrite fashion, "Miss Francis, please excuse this extra nuisance but I thought you might have some insight."

"Not at all, my dear Captain, not at all. Now you see – I'm beginning to talk like him. Pretty soon I'll be calling you Navarre."

"You'll be calling me what?"

"Never mind."

"But – what do you make of him?"

"Not sure, crackpot or psycho. Maybe both, an obsessed fan, perhaps. In either case, probably – no probably about it – obviously not the genuine killer."

"C*laro que no.*"

"But it's uncanny. He had the looks, tone of voice, and mannerisms, the raised eyebrow, even the favorite phrases of John Barrymore. But, whoever this Portnofoy character is, for all his panache, he can't be

John Barrymore; he's too robust, healthy looking and mentally alert, among other things."

"A curious development indeed."

"What will you do with him?"

"We'll question him a little more, who knows, we may learn something of actual value from him. He seems to be, as you say, a well-informed fan. Then we'll have to let him go."

She walked back to the hotel in leisurely fashion, lost in thought. Yes, the strange little man was a mental case or fanatical devotee, perhaps both, but there was something compelling, and disturbing, about her most curious encounter with him. She couldn't shake the feeling it was somehow related to the case at hand, but in what way she didn't know. One thing she was certain of, however: his pompous self-confession didn't convince. No, there was something else about this encounter she found unsettling.

CHAPTER 6

Johnny Caballero approached the tall, imposing iron gates which served as the entrance to Warner Brothers. The attendant – his badge said his name was John Hardee – was an old man with a crinkled face who looked like he'd been with the company for decades. Caballero showed him the note, and the man had a look at it, reading with obvious interest.

"Miss Francis? Her word is always good enough for me." He gestured to a uniformed security guard to come over to the gate. "Please escort Mr. Caballero to Mr. Flynn's room."

The guard and Caballero walked through two blocks of barricks-like structures, then proceeded through a maze of buildings, sets and alleyways on their way to the stars' quarters. Much as Flynn was a fast rising property at the studio, he was not yet cinematic royalty of the highest rank and accordingly his bungalow style dressing room facility was comfortable but not lavish, and this was reflected in the simple, spartan architecture. The guard knocked at the door. "Mr. Flynn, there's a gentleman here to see you. Says it's important."

"Then shoo him in, old boy, shoo him in."

The guard opened the door then disappeared. Johnny entered and saw Flynn sitting at a typewriter, his fingers tapping away at the keys, a look of intense concentration on his face. He was casually dressed in a sports shirt, slacks and sandals. There were manuscript pages strewn about. Since Johnny had heard of Flynn's literary ambitions he wasn't especially surprised.

Flynn looked up and said, "It's this damned book I'm working on, you know – seems it'll never end. It's about memories of the good old, I'm tempted to say happier days, sailing in the South Seas with roughneck pals. But it's the very devil to get it down in words. I think I'll call it *Beam Ends*. What do you think?"

Bemused, Johnny simply offered, "Sounds good to me."

"But what can I do for you? I didn't catch your name."

"Johnny Caballero, sir."

The Flynn smile, with lots of teeth. "Johnny Caballero. I've heard of you; you're a friend of Kay's."

"Yes, I am. Speaking of Kay, I've something for you she insisted I give to you personally." He handed Flynn the sealed envelope. He opened it and looked over the contents, and his face brightened as he sported one of his trademark roguish grins.

"So it looks like Kay has a little homework for me."

"Anything I can help with?" Johnny asked his

question with more rhetorical duty than enthusiasm.

"No, I don't believe so; I've my own sources. But keep yourself close, just in case. This will be a welcome break from this blasted book and, since I get a few days off from shooting tomorrow, it's good timing all around. My love to Kay. Tell her I'll be sailing down to Mazatlán in a couple of days with my results."

Johnny then excused himself and left Mr. Flynn's bungalow. Much as it would have been flattering to work for a man of Mr. Flynn's calibre, he had plenty of his own homework to do and he reminded himself he couldn't waste any time getting to it.

Johnny warily eyed the grey nondescript structure from the sidewalk. The corporate office of Far West Publishing was located near Hollywood and Cahuenga Boulevards in a solid four story office building built long before the Deco era. Thus it displayed a rather grand imperial style popular in the Twenties and earlier. He entered the building in a gingerly fashion, trying to be as inconspicuous as possible. He then walked up the stairs to just outside the main office, taking a seat unobtrusively in the mezzanine area where he could monitor the activities. He noticed a smartly tailored, pert brunette sitting at her desk at the outer edges of the inner sanctum. From what he could tell Far West pretty much had the third floor to themselves, and everything was humming with activity. He noticed lots of people coming and going. He even thought he might have recognized one of the authors, yet another mystery writer looking de rigueur disheveled and vaguely alcoholic. Johnny's well trained eyes made it easy for him to tell who were the literary types and who were the business types. If any of them were saddened by Miss Wembley's passing he couldn't see any trace of it. This would be a challenge, entering the sacred gates and getting his hands on the hot material, but he thought he was up to the task.

Miss Francis had one or two more individuals on her list of preliminary interviews. Before seeing the suspicious Miss Luckingham, she wanted to talk to one Buck LaRue. She'd read his rather bland police report but wished to follow up and accordingly had arranged an appointment with him for mid-afternoon in the hotel lobby.

She walked up to where he was sitting and thought she must have the wrong man: he looked more like a banker from Indianapolis, or some such place, than a writer of raucous Westerns, which she'd heard was his forte. He was perhaps thirty-five years old, and like all the men writers she'd met here, wore a suit, in his case a plain brown suit. He was ordinary looking with a chuffy face and he wore round spectacles which didn't seem to help him much as his eyes squinted when he looked at her. He rose from his chair and greeted her with a mechanical, "Miss Francis, truly an honor."

"So very nice to meet you, Mr. LaRue." After preliminaries she began with a somewhat off-topic question. "Please satisfy my curiosity about your name."

"Yes, of course, I get lots of comments about it. Well, I thought Buck LaRue had a better sounding pedigree than Quintin Throckmorton, my real name. Somehow it just seemed more like a writer of

Westerns."

"It certainly does. But what are you doing at a mystery writers' conference?"

"Yes, strange, isn't it? Well, I wanted to, how does one say, expand my horizons, and incorporate a few mystery techniques in my novels. You see, being a writer of trashy Westerns allows me to pay the bills, barely, but it gets awfully tiresome, writing the same thing over and over. The group was gracious enough to allow me to attend, as a guest. In return I agreed to submit a modest donation to their young writer's scholarship fun. You've heard of it?"

"No, not really." She paused and stared straight ahead, in thought. She could hear the faint sound of piano music wafting in from the nearby bar. The tune was *Embraceable You.*

LaRue looked at her, a little puzzled, but he filled in the conversational vacuum. "Well, anyway, I don't know much about the writers here, their secrets and all that, but I wanted to talk to you about something I heard the other night, a conversation that might be of significance, which I left out of my official summary for the police."

"Why so?"

"Oh, I suppose I didn't want to cast suspicion on anyone unnecessarily."

"Please, Mr. LaRue, or Rockmorton, there's plenty of suspicion and motive to go around, so what is it you have?"

"Well, last night, I was sitting over there – " he said, gesturing in a cornerly direction. "A large fanned palm was next to me and, per usual, I don't think anyone noticed my presence. My nondescript personality, you know."

"Yes?" Miss Francis's tone was inquisitive but cautious.

"Well, what I heard, or thought I heard – everything was sort of vague ..."

"Please! Out with it."

"Well, I was sitting almost flush against the thin glass partition that separates the bar from the lobby, and I could hear voices from the bar, on the other side of the glass, lots of different voices, sort of murmurings. But two were close enough to stand out and catch a little of what they were saying. Loud voices, two distinct personalities. What I heard was muffled and what with the music and other people talking I couldn't make out everything, but there was a man's voice and a woman's voice, that much I know. The man's accent was English, cockney, lower class, forceful, sort of baritone. He spoke fast, so did the woman.

"The man said where were you last night, no welching, you said you'd be here with the money. Listen, I kept my end of the bargain, scrounging those two muscle men for you. Then the woman said something like what are you talking about, and don't be so loud, you'll attract attention. And she said stop threatening me or I'll go to the police. Then the man said, police, you're a good one to talk, quit stalling, you know what I'm talking about; if you don't pay up I'll spill the beans – or worse, if you get my message. The woman's voice then said something like, oh very well, meet me tonight down at the beach by the flagpole."

"The man sounds like Mr. Thrugg, the bartender."

"I don't know him, but I've heard the others talk of him. Sounds like he could be the man."

Miss Francis lifted her hand and rubbed the side of her face, in thought. "Yes, it certainly does." Another pause, then, "Did you actually see them?"

"No, I'm afraid not. Of course," he continued, "it could all be totally innocent; maybe the gentleman and lady were simply having a friendly argument, a misunderstanding, something like that. And if it really was nefarious, would they do something so suspicious as meeting out in the open?"

"Sometimes the most public places are the best for doing something you want to hide. And be assured this Mr. Thrugg is no gentleman. But was there anything else you remember about the conversation, the way they spoke, accents, whatever?"

"As I said the man spoke with an English lower class accent, the woman's voice was … nondescript. I didn't recognize it; it wasn't anyone from the writers' group, not that I could tell anyway. But I can't be sure exactly."

Miss Francis began to get up from the table. "It's been a great help, really. Not to be abrupt, but I must be off. My many thanks, Mr. LaRue; your comments have been most illuminating."

She had to get outside. A lot of new information to digest. She walked across the street and began to stroll along the malecón, and the sounds from the crashing waves helped to soothe her confused and busy thoughts. What the devil could Buck LaRue's account mean? Maybe it was all innocent, as he had theorized, but Henry Thrugg was not the picture of innocence. Apparently this woman had hired him to arrange for the body to be moved upstairs and was stiffing him on the payment. And the woman must have been the murderer, or at least involved in some way in the murder. But who was it? And why? And what was the connection? If Mr. LaRue's description of the voice was correct, it couldn't have been any of the writers. But then again he didn't sound very sure about exactly what he'd heard.

As for Mr. LaRue, what was he doing at a conference that was mostly social? Somehow his explanation he was here to learn mystery writing techniques just didn't convince.

Otherwise she wasn't getting anywhere with the rest of the so-called suspects, all of them vaguely suspicious but nothing concrete about them she could put her finger on. In semi-desperation her mind began to wander: she thought again about that crazy self-confessed character. Yes, Captain Seguro agreed with her initial opinion, but was it possible – did she need to take another look at him; was there something to his bizarre story after all? This whole business was beginning to give her a huge headache. And she never wanted to be a detective anyway. *Give me a good movie! With a good script, that makes sense. Something I understand.* She walked some more, lost in thought and eagerly awaiting the reports of her two aces in the hole, Johnny Caballero and Errol Flynn.

The hotel's palm garden flowed out of the elegant, spacious lobby, and Miss Francis sat in one of the plush cozy chairs. There she awaited the arrival of her next, perhaps last interviewee, the heiress apparent herself. The lush greenery and landscaping seduced with its extravagance and perfumed sensuousness; there must have been thousands of plants, trees and flowers.

Livistona Palms, Frangipanis, Traveller's Palms,
Casuarina Trees, Heliconias, Bird of Paradise, Cyas,
Petunias in hanging baskets, Ixora and Flame Trees,
Peacock Flowers, Lantana Camarablooms,
Bouganvillas, Hibiscus. They were all there.

Taking a page out of Mr. LaRue's book, she
chose a place in a corner that was partially obscured by
one of the large palms. There she awaited her audience
with Miss L with a mixture of curiosity and anxiety. As
an author of mystery novels, Claire Luckingham was
nowhere near as well known as Miss Wembley; Miss
Francis had heard of her but not read any of her books.
And despite Percy Doveless's admonitions, she was
skeptical there was anything very sinister about Miss
Luckingham. But now her thoughts were more on what
Mr. LaRue had said about Mr. Thrugg and the
mysterious woman. But who was this woman, and what
could have been her motive?

Then she noticed her subject, who walked into the
garden with a flourish. Claire Luckingham looked the
part of the new queen of mystery writers: fiftyish, tall,
statuesque, aristocratic, with fine, knowing hazel blue
eyes, a full, voluptuous figure, high cheekbones, and
something of a snub nose which hinted of a Slavic
background. She had a generous mouth with thick red
lips, large, perfectly symmetrical teeth, and pale skin to
which heavy makeup had been applied and apparently
hadn't taken in any of the famous local sun. She was
resplendent in a full length, chalk colored Grecian style
Madame Grès evening dress that was more of a gown,
topped with a white, rounded Casablanca felt wide
brimmed hat with white velvet bow, and absurd long
white gloves. It was as though she had to upstage the

famous actress and well known fashion plate who was to interview her, but her clothes suggested more of Mae West than the well-heeled sophisticate she desperately wanted to be. In any case, she needn't have gone to all the trouble to outdo Miss Francis, who wore a simple white outfit that hinted of a tennis suit with its blouse and knee length skirt and white shoes.

After the polite introductory formalities, Miss Francis ran through her usual litany of preliminary comments and questions. Both women were on the verge of boredom when Miss Luckingham dropped a bit of a bombshell.

"I think you'd do well to take another look at Mr. Favell and Miss Wentworth."

"In what way?"

"Hadn't you heard, darling – " It was a breathy *dahling* in a languidly affected Tallulah Bankhead manner, but then again everything about Miss Luckingham was a bit affected, the ersatz British manner, mid Atlantic accent, and European chic clothes. However, the elegant facade barely managed to obscure a brassy American straightforwardness and ordinariness.

"They had some nasty business with Miss Wembley a few years ago," she continued, pausing with obvious relish to savor the moment, looking in both directions as if to check no one was listening in. "They were just starting out as a mystery writing team, and sent the sketch for one of their novels to her for encouragement, critiquing and all that, and wouldn't you know it, she stole the whole thing, lock, stock and barrel, and adapted it for one of her novels. They made a terrible stink of it, threatened to go to the papers and make it public. Ultimately there was some sort of settlement, very hush hush."

Miss Luckingham luxuriated in the attention she was getting from her famous companion; she looked as though she'd been preparing – even expecting – this moment; the prize was now finally hers and the wait was over. She continued her story. "In the meantime he's had to scrimp together a life as a second rate script writer for B movies, and she, well, she suffered an even worse fate, making do as a part-time librarian over at UCLA and doing various odd jobs editing and typing. They are the classic literary social climbers, if you ask me."

"That's extremely interesting, and potentially most incriminating." Miss Francis tilted her head in an inquisitive pose. "But how does it happen you know of it?"

At her most coy, Miss Luckingham affected a conspiratorial smile and said, "You know how word gets around in these closed circles. Anyway I thought you'd be interested in the story. As to why they are here, it's anybody's guess – they never attended any of the other writer conferences. Maybe they were trying to shake her down for a few more dollars. Maybe they wanted to do her in just for good measure and see she gets what's coming to her … oops! I mustn't be so direct in speaking my mind. And, by the way, that sort of reminds me, she and I liked our practical jokes. The colorful incident at the restaurant the other night – I'm sure you've heard about it from the others – making me the top suspect and all that. Just a comedy of manners, I assure you. You see, she and I weren't the best of friends, I'll grant you that, but we liked putting one over on the others now and then, just to keep them guessing."

"Yes, I suppose it would bring a certain amount of satisfaction, wouldn't it?"

Perhaps sensing the hint of sarcasm in Miss Francis's voice, Miss Luckingham didn't respond to her remark but instead looked away.

At that time a small man in a police uniform approached Miss Francis hesitatingly and said, "Your regrets, my lady, interrupt. The Captain, he ask I to give you to this."

He handed her an envelope, and she opened it.

Miss Francis, A good development to report, of a sort. Henry Thrugg has been located, but he's not going to give us much information. His body was found washed up on the rocks down by where the divers perform, just beyond Olas Altas beach. Foul play definitely with three gun shots to chest. Preliminary tests suggest the gun used to shoot Mr. Thrugg is the same that was used to kill Miss Wembley. With regards, Capt. S.

"Miss Luckingham, you'll have to excuse me."

"Quite all right," she said tentatively. She couldn't hide her disappointment her all too brief audience was over.

Miss Francis walked pensively across the grounds and went into the hotel lobby. She stood there, and her eyes blankly took in the surroundings. She wasn't quite sure of her next move, in fact she was getting tired of the entire affair.

Then she heard the front desk man say, "Miss Francis, Miss Francis."

"Yes, what is it?"

"A telephone call, long distance, from California.

You can take it in the little office behind the front counter."

She walked behind the counter, into the office and picked up the phone. "Mr. Caballero from Los Angeles," the operator's voice said.

"Yes, go ahead."

"Kay, it's Johnny."

"Johnny, what have you got?"

"Well, lots of good stuff. I was able to sneak into the publishing office last night." He spoke rapidly as he delivered the words.

She took his agitated speech as a hopeful sign, but was cautious. "How did you manage that?"

"A little help from the office secretary. She couldn't resist the Johnny C charm. The two hundred dollar bribe helped, too. I'm afraid I'm running up my expense account something awful."

"Don't worry about the expenses. Well, what did you find out?"

"The novel was a pure bust. I read the manuscript cover to cover, pretty deadly, well, not bad really, just not much of a mystery novel, not as much fun as her others. Lots of jumping around in time and pompous philosophizing from a down and out, alcoholic hero, but anyway, I didn't see anything there someone would kill over."

"That's too bad; the novel was one of the few good leads. So Percy was right after all," she mumbled.

"What was that about Percy?"

"Never mind. Anything else?"

"Actually, I might have something good."

"What's that?"

"It's something the secretary said, things she

overheard her boss at the publishing house talking about, that Miss Wembley had a curious revision style, and she didn't know much about her own stories when he asked her details about plot, logic, that sort of thing, not even about her series character Mr. Clive Baxter. She always said she'd have to check her notes and get back with him. He never much minded; her stories always came out right in the end, and sold well. He just explained it away that she was one of these eccentric author types who had to do things their own way.

"And by the way, a little bonus, as I was browsing through the file cabinets for anything interesting I came across a legal document from a few years ago, a settlement of a sort. Between Miss Wembley and a certain author team you'll appreciate, Jack Favell and Catherine Wentworth. It seems Miss Wembley pinched one of their stories and used it as the basis for one of her own novels. They sued her over it, settled for $5,000, no admission of guilt, nothing revealed publicly. Everyone seemed to be happy. Oh, and here's the kicker: the signature on the bottom of the page for the lawyer who drew up the settlement, one Mr. Harrison Tumworth."

The old walrus. He didn't say a thing about this. "Yes, I'd heard as much, only hearsay, but not the part about Tumworth's involvement or the details of the settlement. Now you've confirmed it as fact. Great work, Johnny."

"Oh, and Mr. Flynn got the message you sent him. He seemed very pleased, said he would sail down on his yacht in a couple of days. As for background information about Miss Wembley, I don't have a lot; she grew up back East, got a degree from a small college in Vermont, started writing mystery novels about ten years ago. About that time she moved out to California. Far West Publishing picked her up and since then, what do they say, the rest is history. One best seller after another at the rate of about one a year.

"Oh, and another thing, I came across a file labelled Percy Doveless, and in it were cancelled checks, not Miss Wembley's checks, but checks cashed *by* her, paid by Mr. Doveless, a hundred dollars a pop, three of them. What was really interesting, though, was what was written in the notes portion of the check. It was 'writing lessons'. How does that grab you? And it gets better. I managed to contact Miss Wembley's maid who comes in and cleans up twice a week. Unfortunately she's Mexican and her comprehension of English is limited. She didn't know too much but said just before the holiday to Mexico she overheard voices, sounded like an argument between Miss Wembley and the secretary, something about getting what she deserves and being generous up to now. She couldn't make out everything but it sounded pretty spicy to me."

"It's all great work, Johnny, really sensational stuff. As always you've earned your keep."

"Shall I come down there?"

"No, stay where you are, I may need you there."

She needed time and space to mull over all she learned from Johnny Caballero and what she thought she might have learned from Claire Luckingham and Buck LaRue. She walked and walked, down her favorite route of Angel Flores to the plaza, then past the cathedral through the mercado, where she stopped to have a look at the Chiapas style clothes which the native women were selling at a stand just outside the back entrance. She bought a handbag of intricate colors and design for a mere ten pesos. The woman who sold it had a deep tan and a wrinkly face but projected a great dignity. While Miss Francis was giving her the money the woman made the sign of the cross three times and she mumbled something about *buena suerte*.

Centro was crowded with postcard sellers, tourist souvenir shops and cafès which spilled out of the buildings around and near the main plaza. She made her way along the narrow, busy streets, at one point giving way to a small procession headed by a band, saint's banner proudly displayed, followed by a small group of women and children with flowers on their way to a nearby shrine.

Miss Francis wandered some more, in this, one of her favorite places in the world to amble and collect one's thoughts. But she couldn't shake the feeling she was being followed. She looked back quickly and noticed a little man dressed in a dark Mexican style business suit. When she looked again he wasn't there. Sometimes she glimpsed him then he would dart away, cat-like. This happened several times.

She was reaching the outer edges of Centro, and was careful to stay on the main road, but from time to time managed surreptitious glances into the small alleyways that she passed. She saw streets which were part paved road, part muck and mud, pigs and dogs scurrying around, and heard noises wafting from old phonographs, and men laughing and singing and strumming their guitars from behind the doors of the *pulquerias* and *cantinas*. She also noticed the odd burro tied to the door while their masters got drunk, and people asleep leaning against the walls, and the occasional child begging.

By now she was thirsty, and also hungry, so she decided to stop at a small café. The name on the outside wall could barely be made out; it seemed to have been hand painted some time ago and it read *La Pequeña Casa Azul.* As was so often the case the place was half home and half restaurant; the living room from the tiny adobe style structure had been converted into the smallest of cantinas with the kitchen off to the side out in the open. The modest peasant house had a scuffed worn tile floor which was nonetheless well swept, and walls consisting of bamboo reeds placed not flush against one another but with a space to afford passage for air. Along the main wall was a large framed print of the Lady of Guadalupe, around which fanned out numerous historical and family photographs. The tall, solidly built young waitress who waited on her wore one of those puffy Yucatan style cotton dresses embroidered along the square neck and bottom hem with colorful designs and flowers.

Miss Francis ordered tortilla soup and a Coke. The soup came with fresh made corn tortillas and a small plate of avocados. It all was tasty and nourishing and served as a nice break from the long walk.

She closed her eyes, then offered a leisurely smile. "*Sabrosa.*" Miss Francis said her word of appreciation with genuine sincerity. The meal cost less than five pesos and this struck her as amazingly inexpensive. Accordingly she left a much larger than necessary tip. She then walked up Zaragoza into a residential neighborhood, wandered a little more and found herself at the Parroquia Cristo Rey, a beautiful elegant structure of blueish trim with two minaret-like spires out front, in its way as grand as the large cathedral near the mercado though much less well known.

She went in and rested for a bit, but thought she glimpsed in the back of the church the same little man who seemed to be following her. He was hovering in the shadows, which obscured her vision and she couldn't get a clear view of him. Still, she pondered, what could it mean? Had someone been sent to spy on her activities, or worse, do her harm? Were any of the outstanding suspects capable of this? If Mr. LaRue's account was indeed accurate, it would place … someone in a most incriminating position, especially in view of Mr. Thrugg's recent demise.

But what about Miss Luckingham; there was something about her, especially her remark about Miss Wembley getting what's coming to her, along with her rather too breezy explanation of her outburst at the restaurant, to say nothing of her too intimate knowledge of Miss Wembley's legal settlement with the Favell-Wentworth writing team. As for Jack Favell and Catherine Wentworth, they certainly had grounds for a grudge with Mavis Wembley, and it could be five thousand dollars just wasn't enough to mollify their sensibilities and give them satisfaction. Maybe they wanted a few more pounds in flesh. And what of Mr. Percy Doveless? Writing lessons with Miss Wembley? He'd hinted of some literary aspirations, but he left the lessons part out in his otherwise fairly candid conversation with her, and in any case, why so few lessons? Was he such a quick study that he had learned everything there was to know? Or was there perhaps some other explanation? Was he hiding something?

Upon arrival back at the *Belmar*, Miss Francis felt at loose ends, confused and fatigued by all the questions and lack of clarity. She walked past the front desk and the attendant said, "This was left for you. Who left it I don't know; it was on the counter." He handed her the envelope. On the front was simply written, *Miss Francis*. Inside was a handwritten note. She did not recognize the handwriting.

If you want to find the answer to your riddle, go to the Casa Floridita, *top of the hill, past the school toward Playa Sur. See the marker on left, the bow.*

It was not signed. She knew there was the possibility of cranks and crackpots but it sounded intriguing enough and she was growing weary from talking to unhelpful witnesses. She began her quest immediately, walking up the hill, past the school and round the curved turn at the top. It felt good to walk, and indeed the directions were accurate. The stylized Cupid's bow sculpture fitted in the white plaster along with the chiseled letters *Casa Floridita* at the gatepost told the visitor he had arrived. The curved gravel drive meandered up between rocks and clumps of agapanthi. The lawn on each side of the driveway looked dry as though the summer sun had scorched it. The drive went past rows of gardens of steep slopes in which there were pruned orange, banana, avocado and lemon trees.

At the end of the drive one reached a large house, square in design with long green shutters, which opened onto a broad terrace overlooking the bay. The large, white two-story house looked much rebuilt and painted the color of undercooked scrambled eggs, arranged around an interior arched courtyard, topped by Spanish Mediterranean tiles. A large garden complemented the keyhole windows, domes and minarets, colonnades and columns. The nearby pool had been dug out of rock in a hillside just below the house, and at one end of the pool was a Bernini style putto through whose mouth water gushed. The Moorish-style setting and furnishings seemed more Roman villa than Sea of Cortez, but there it was.

There was no doorbell; everything was so tranquil the footsteps alone were enough to alert the residents or servants. On the lintel above the entrance was another, carved Cupid's Bow.

She knocked at the main front entrance to the house, but no answer. The door was already ajar, and she let herself in. The house seemed empty, and reeked of cigar and cigarette smoke which clung to the walls and furnishings like heavy moss in a swampy marsh, the dank smell curiously intermixed with a hint of mimosa fragrance. The inside was not lit and rays of sun peeked through the thick, drawn curtain, revealing a heavy overlay of lint and dust which floated in the air like a soupy London fog.

The large drawing room had a fireplace of Yucatan stone, over which a gilded silver owl spread its wings. Two tables were piled high with books, and the main room had a small Steinway grand with vintage sheet music and photographs scattered on and near the piano. There were still more books on shelves which rimmed the perimeter. The eighteenth century Spanish furniture and gilded wooden chandeliers gave the great room a truly grand flavor. French windows at either end of the room led to a front patio and the grounds which afforded one a commanding view of the bay. There was a second house, presumably for servants, discreetly tucked away in the back, barely visible from the main structure.

The entrance hall had a blue tile floor which led past a large Kuan Yin statue which in turn led to an elegantly ornate iron staircase the type of which they do so well in Mexico. Miss Francis noticed a fondness for Chinese and Indian sculptures; every room had at least one Kuan Yin and one Buddha of varying sizes, eras and styles. The dining room was small and high ceilinged and could sit eight, though in this case dinner was set for six; perhaps the lady of the house was expecting guests. Miss Francis recognized the fine English silver from Phillips on Bond Street, and the silver *sous-plats* with large ducal crests.

As she explored the premises, she noticed all sorts of objects d'art: African masks, stuffed animals, cubist paintings, pre-Columbian Mexican sculpture and most of all photographs. They were everywhere, mostly of the lady of the house, of her alone as well as with various famous personages. Then she thought she glimpsed the figure of a man through the main room windows. He resembled the little man who had followed her around town earlier, but alas he quickly slipped away before she could get a good look.

She continued to explore, to the upstairs. Ultimately she saw seven, or was it eight, bedrooms and five baths. The mistress's bedroom was a corner room on the second floor, with a view of the sea and a marble fireplace. The large Italianate bed had flowers painted on the headboard and footboard, and it was set at an angle at which one could get the best light, and behind it stood a French classic era sculpture. A bookcase was built into the wall which contained an impressive collection of mostly antiquarian tomes: first editions, series, eighteenth and nineteenth century French, German and Spanish encyclopedias, the *Britannica* Eleventh, the complete works of Goethe, Cervantes, Chekhov, Ibsen and Shakespeare and, curiously, Mark Twain.

On the mantelpiece and spread all over the wall were photographs of the lady in full theatrical regalia and with various celebrities and other worthies. In most of the photos she was adorned in Edwardian or Art Nouveau dress of full length hems, corsets and high collars, her long hair inevitably wrapped up, all highly theatrical. The large, now long out of fashion hats with plumage, lots of feathers and flowers, the clothes with their puffed out sleeves, narrow waist, and prominent bust and posterior were thought to be the ideal of a desirable woman fifty years ago. However, they were a far cry from the streamlined, Deco-influenced fashions which were such a critical element of Miss Francis's chic, modern look. In a pleasing coincidence she noticed one picture, probably decades old, of the lady posing with theatrical and society types, and she would have sworn one of the persons was Somerset Maugham. Miss Francis wondered whether the answer to her riddle, as promised in the note, would be found in these musty photographs, books or other memorabilia.

She walked into the guest bedrooms, and noticed the shuttered windows opened upon row after row of orange, lemon and mango trees. Any number of exotic birds sang and the honeysuckle and mimosa bloomed, exuding a most seductive fragrance. The wind periodically wheezed through crevices in the walls and windows, creating a mournful, moaning sort of sound, reinforcing the impression one got from the house – its undeniable beauty and grandeur notwithstanding – of an indescribable sadness and nostalgia.

She walked back downstairs and noticed a small, thin, impeccably dressed man near the door, and she intuited immediately he was not the same man who had been following her.

"Oh, hello," she said.

"Hello, Miss Francis."

"You know me," she said.

"Of course, but permit me to introduce myself, I'm Pierre, the butler." He was a wiry man of maybe forty-five years, rather small, with delicate, Levantine features, and he spoke serviceable, if slightly accented English. "Your presence is a great pleasure, but may I inquire as to the reason for this visit?"

"I received this note and it made me curious. Maybe you can enlighten me as to the author, or the where and how I may find the answer to my riddle."

She showed him the note and he read it. A hint of a smile pierced the corners of his mouth. "To the best of my knowledge, no one from here sent such a message to you. You see, most of the staff is away and I did not send any such note. Perhaps Miss Francis is the victim of a practical joke, or maybe the author of the note has a different purpose in mind other than your investigation."

"You know about that too?"

A nod in the affirmative. "Yes. I'm afraid news travels fast in Mazatlán."

"But whose house it this? And is the lady at home?"

"Regretfully, no. Miss Townsend is traveling in Europe, as she does this time of year."

"Who is Miss Townsend?"

"Miss Norma Townsend was an important stage actress, in mostly New York and London, around the turn of the century and somewhat beyond. She never appeared in films, and retired here some years ago. She lives here about six months a year, in semi-reclusive style, though she has occasional visitors from the North and has a small coterie of friends here in Mazatlán."

"Yes, I've heard of her, but had no idea she lived here. I regret I am not one of her circle of friends, not yet at least; she sounds a fascinating woman. "

"Did you know she once danced the tango with Douglas Fairbanks right here in the main room, on this very tile, some years ago of course. She was almost a mentor to him in his young days, before he became the great film star."

"Most impressive. But about my being sent here, what do you make of it?"

"A mystery, isn't it? Perhaps the contents of the note is not related to the investigation of the author's death. A warning perhaps, the fragility of fame, all glory is fleeting – " He looked away. "But I say too much already. I leave you now. Please, do have a further look around. Just be careful about touching things."

"Thanks, most generous of you."

She did have a look around, but only for a few minutes. By this time she was self-conscious about her presence. She left the great house and walked back towards the hotel. From the top of the hill she could see the vista of the beach spread out before her in its natural glory. So the tip about the *Casa* had been a prank after all, maybe; the note only said she'd find the answer to her riddle, nothing specific about the case. Who could have sent the thing?

She felt frustrated but also privileged to play the voyeur and to have seen the great lady's home. Then she mused over Pierre the butler's gentle warnings on the merits of an eccentric, reclusive life in a tomb by the sounding sea.

It was late afternoon and Miss Francis needed a different kind of break, so she permitted herself the modest indulgence of a visit to the *Belmar's* elegant, blue tiled, yellow filagree inlaid swimming pool – after all she *was* here on holiday. For her swimsuit she chose a bright red, stretch-rayon one piece that accented her dark hair and moreover showed off her evenly tanned *café au lait* skin tones and her gamine yet athletic silhouette. As she walked into the pool area all the men's eyes – and a few of the women's – turned in her direction.

Walking along the side of the pool she saw hummingbirds hovering over the bougainvillea and hibiscus blossoms nearby. The water in the pool was clear and gentle, and she could see the bottom as she passed on her way to one of the pool's cushion-stuffed reclining chairs. As was her custom she looked over the people nearby. She recognized Mr. LaRue, lounging back, his face partially covered by a towel. Also an overweight Mexican gentleman of advanced years, a family of four, and a couple, newlyweds possibly, and finally one, youngish woman, a real beauty, a fellow film star perhaps on retreat.

But the person who stood out most was an elegant, senior lady who just then entered the pool area. What was the old saying, she acted as if she owned the place, and maybe she did. Perhaps she simply lived at the *Belmar*. In any case, with her rather haughty carriage and precise movements, it was obvious she was right at home. Her dark, large sunglasses, fine jewelry, and long silver hair which she wore pulled back gave her a vaguely severe aura but also a sense of mystery. She was accompanied by her young, handsome servant of perhaps twenty-five years. The young man was possibly a nurse of some sort; he wore a white uniform.

The lady was of a certain age, seventy-five, maybe eighty, and had a finely chiseled face with a beak nose. She methodically undid her gossamer pink robe, revealing a tiny two-piece swimsuit of bright green with purple trim which barely covered a burnished brown, skinny figure of maybe ninety pounds soaking wet. Indeed there was little meat left on her bones. But most important was her demeanor; she didn't care who was watching, or what they thought.

She carried herself with such an aristocratic bearing; even at this chronological remove, somehow her onetime beauty shone through. Yes, she was still beautiful and in her way physically impressive, all the more so when she dove into the water and began to swim laps. Miss Francis lost count after the lady had gotten to five laps, and accordingly she returned to the comforting refuge of her book. A few pages later she looked up and the lady was gone. She closed her eyes, feeling sleepy from the reading and the sun. Just before she fell asleep she could hear the faint purring of the hummingbirds near the flowers.

Finally it was dinner time, and as she was rather tired, Miss Francis chose to have her meal at the hotel restaurant and retire early. She chose a table far away from the rest of the customers and listened to the mariachi music drifting in from outside. The strolling musicians performed with panache and ardor, and although she did not recognize the pieces, much less know the names of them, she did hear in the sounds the sun and the trees and the grand haciendas, formally dressed squires in *charro* suits serenading ladies, the spirit of the priest going to the church and praying, the Spanish missionaries celebrating the Christian feast days, the dancing in the fiestas and weddings and baptisms, images of confetti, firecrackers and the Virgin, and of revelers holding their tequila glasses and singing along with a power in the music that bespoke of other, more courtly but also more earthy times. She also smelt in her nostrils a warm scent of the Mexican farm soil and a hint of freshly caught fish and became conscious of being in touch with primitive forces in mother earth and the sea, an elemental power with roots deep in nature with no home in geography.

She had a look around at the fellow customers, and from where she was, she could glimpse Mr. Tumworth tucked away on the far side of the room, having what looked like a conspiratorial meal with a companion, a nattily dressed gentleman whom she hadn't seen before. Probably a lawyer, she thought. The man was about forty, tall, wiry, with a pale complexion, clothed in the obligatory grey suit, his thinning brown hair receding from a pallid forehead that shone like polished china. His eyes, like those of Mr. Tumworth, were remarkable for their sharp intensity, but also for their coldness. The two men spoke in hushed whispers amid glances around them as if to make sure no one was listening in, their discourses only periodically punctuated by bits of wheezy laughter, noticeable for the touch of self-satisfied cruelty undeniably present in the otherwise innocuous chuckles.

Then the man began to clutch his throat and the collar of his shirt as if having some kind of attack. He fell out of his chair down on the floor and began to twitch all over and his body shook and his legs kicked back and forth. His face turned pink, then purple.

"Please, quick, an ambulance!" Mr. Tumworth said in a loud voice all the more remarkable for him since he usually spoke in hushed tones.

Some of the customers stood up and walked over toward the man, and the *maître* and several waiters rushed over to table.

"Is there a doctor here?"

A distinguished looking gentleman made his way forward "Yes, I'm a doctor," he said. He proceeded to examine the man, who had stopped moving. The ambulance arrived in just a few minutes and they whisked the gentleman away, the doctor close by in the vehicle.

By this time Miss Francis had made her way over to speak to Mr. Tumworth. "What do you make of it?"

"Not sure." His voice quivered and his pallor was still a bit pale. "I've never seen anything like this; looks all the world like an attack of epilepsy, but I'm not aware he had the condition."

"Who is the gentleman, if it's not too inquisitive to ask." Miss Francis was polite, but persistent.

"His name is Gordon Craig. He's with the legal department at Far West Publishing. He came down here to discuss a few technical points arising from Miss Wembley's unfortunate demise." He held his hand up in a blocking manner. "And, no, I'm not at liberty to discuss any of the specifics."

"Couldn't it have waited until you got back?"

A long breath. "Let's just say there were some significant matters to deal with that really couldn't wait."

"Isn't it a bit suspicious; do you expect foul play?"

Another raised, open palm. "Miss Francis, as I said before my job is not to solve cases but look out for my client once he's been charged. As for theories of who did what to whom, I'm afraid that's your department."

"Something to do with the new book, perhaps?"

Another deep breath; Tumworth's impatience was beginning to show. "I can only tell you Mr. Craig was a most harmless individual in a low keyed job, an attorney in name only; in reality he functioned more like an accountant. Really I don't see any reason why someone would want to kill him."

All perfectly logical and well spoken, as Tumworth always was. But Miss Francis had her doubts.

CHAPTER 7

Errol Flynn's 75-foot twin-masted yacht, the *Sirocco*, dwarfed the small fishing boats and other vessels in the bay. The gleamingly polished schooner seemed a mirage in the little harbor, its two main beams reaching heavenward as though striving for the infinite. Miss Francis walked briskly toward the boat and as she approached waved to Flynn. He waved back and bounded off the yacht with his signature dégagé flair which hinted of the ballet dancer he might have been, but also spoke of the amateur prize fighter, tennis champion and all-around athlete which was.

Flynn was in good form as he walked briskly with a spontaneous exuberance and infectious joy of living which all, sometimes even Miss Francis, found hard to resist. He smiled broadly and gave her a warm hug. "Kay, dear, always a pleasure; how is it you're more beautiful and radiant every time I see you?"

A skeptical smile. "I think you exaggerate a bit, Errol, but thanks all the same; you're always the charmer, aren't you? But this is all business. What do you have for me?"

"Why don't we walk a bit," he said. And they did, strolling along the malecón. They stopped and sat on one of the little benches which rimmed the walkway. Locals had seen movie stars before, and Flynn was a regular visitor, thus happily there were no autograph hounds or curiosity seekers and they could converse in private. The sun shone brightly and the high tide waves rolled in and thundered with authority, creating a pleasing obligato to the conversation.

"By the way, how *are* you?" she said. "You're looking great."

"Thanks, it's good to hear; I try to take care of myself. Anyway, my book progresses, and in a couple of months they begin shooting *Robin Hood*, which should be fun. But Lili's being problematic as usual and Curtiz is the very devil to work with. Sometimes I think I would be happier as a beach bum in Australia or New Guinea or some such place. The sea and sailing are my true loves, no disrespect to the opposite sex, especially present company."

"You've always had a touch of the poet about you, haven't you? That and a flair for intrigue and adventure. That's why I was sure I could rely on your help. Now give. What did you find out?"

"Well, most of my sources were legitimate, even if my methods weren't. Greasing the palms, that sort of thing. But some of the more unsavory contacts were found through my sailing chums in Mexico. I've gotten to know some pretty rough types, you know. They were enlightening as to your Mr. Thrugg, and yes, I heard about his untimely, or perhaps I should say timely demise."

"Okay, Errol, I'm sufficiently impressed; you have criminals for friends. Now get to it. What about Mr. Thrugg?"

"Well, to begin with, it seems his name wasn't Thrugg at all, but as far as we can tell he was one Jock O'Halloran, an English/Irish gent with a long criminal record in the UK. He skipped bail awaiting a murder trial there and disappeared to the States, where he changed his name and appearance and made a living of sorts, mostly as a small time thief, and sometimes venturing into big time confidence schemes. The Feds were just about to put the sting on him – they weren't quite sure whether they'd hold him on charges or send him back to their English cousins, who had first dibs on him. Anyway he slipped away and came to Mazatlán, where he's been hiding out practically in plain sight, planning his next move. But even here, with all the vagaries of the extradition laws he was never totally safe."

Miss Francis rubbed her hand on the side of her face in thought. "Apparently the killer must have held something pretty threatening over him to get him to go along with such a hair-brained scheme as moving a dead body up to my suite."

"That, or dangling a handsome amount of money in front of him, or both. As for our late actress Miss Leah Lavish, her real name was Mary Hoover – not quite so romantic, is it? – from Akron, Ohio, talk of unromantic. Anyway, she was salt of the earth, born into a lower class family of factory workers but with her own ideas of worldly success. Along the way she did some local repertory theater and small time nightclub work. Her specialty was mime and sometimes she worked as a magician and male impersonator. But her real love was crime; her last charge was felonious assault, robbery and attempted murder. It looked all the world like they had her dead to rights but she was able to slither out of it on a technicality. She thought better of staying in Ohio and sought the greener pastures of California. So she did odd jobs to support herself financially and eventually got some bit parts in theater, after that landing a minor contract over at Universal. But her career didn't really go anywhere and that pretty much bring us up to date on her."

Miss Francis paused to look downward, somewhat mesmerized by the symphony of nature below. The surf roared intermittently into the V-shaped canyon like a rip tide, smothering the bare rocks with white foam, then spewing up geyser-like, and thundering back into the ocean, leaving the rocks as bare as before. In a short time the entire process would repeat itself.

"That's very illuminating, Errol, and sort of fits in with some of my own theories."

"Glad to hear that. By the way, I heard Tumworth's in town. The old fox, costs me a fortune in fees but he's good to have around in a pinch, if you know what I mean. Is he behaving himself?"

"In a manner of speaking, I suppose. Cantankerous as ever, but helpful, in his way."

Flynn didn't respond to what she said, but, rather, hitting his rhetorical stride, flashed an impish smile as he continued, "I'm tempted to say something like I saved the best for last – but I won't. Let's just say you'll find it ... fascinating."

"Well?"

"It's the loyal secretary, Miss Kathleen Niffin. She grew up in a comfortable, eminently respectable if not quite wealthy Rhode Island family. She got her Master's degree from Wellesley College, in English Literature. Oh, and I've got to tell you this, her thesis was titled *An Examination of the Regressive Tendencies in the Early Fiction of Mary Roberts Rinehart*. Quite a mouthful, isn't it?"

Miss Francis hesitated for a moment, then thought, it may well be more than that, a motive for murder possibly, but she kept her suspicions to herself.

Flynn continued, "Then about ten years ago she met Miss Wembley, and the two of them simply fell in love with each other, in a sisterly sort of way, as far as I can tell. They moved out to California, a good career move as it turns out for Miss Wembley but quite the comedown for Miss Niffin, wouldn't you say, given her qualifications."

Miss Francis stared ahead. Then she said rather tentatively, "Yes, that would definitely be the case, if it really was a comedown."

"How's that?"

"I'll explain later. Go on."

"But oh, here's the topper, and this one I had to literally pay for in gold, well, not quite gold, but lots of fresh, crisp, hundred dollar bills. We took a look at her bank statements from 1930 till the present, and in the past seven years there have been a thousand dollars a month deposited into her account, source of funds unknown. Quite the generous amount for a secretary's salary, wouldn't you say?"

"Yes I would say. That's truly sensational, Errol. I've got a feeling I know who made the deposits. This person was not the source of the money, though. I've got my ideas on that. But have to run now, darling. As they say, time may be of the essence."

Jaw slightly dropped, Flynn balked; women didn't usually run away from him, very much the contrary. But he regained his focus and said, "Happy to be of service, dearest Kay. I'll linger on for a day or two, then I'll have to get back. I'm meeting up tonight with some pals of mine and we're doing the town, strictly a man's night out; should be fun." Flynn always had a smooth explanation even for disappointment but she was glad he had an out. He began to trundle off in the direction of his yacht.

"Just don't get too rowdy," Miss Francis cautioned.

Flynn turned around, open arms imploring, "Kay, you know me."

"Yes, I know you – oh, never mind … have a good time in Mazatlán."

She walked away and considered her conversation with Flynn. It was all beginning to make sense. She didn't quite have every piece of the puzzle securely in place, but she was getting close. Which reminded her, it was time for one more chat with a not so revealing witness, a Mr. Harrison Tumworth.

CHAPTER 8

This time her tone and general demeanor was sterner, even accusatory. "Now, Mr. Tumworth – "

As always, Tumworth was the model of British decorum and unflappability. "Please, I insist … it's Harrison, or simply Harris." He pronounced the words with his usual calm delivery and controlled, well modulated tones.

"All right … Harrison." She thought it sounded little short of ridiculous but went along anyway. "However, I must press you about some new bits of information I've discovered, which, looked at in a certain way, may throw a slightly different light on things. It brings up the inevitable question of why you weren't more forthcoming in my first talk with you."

"Yes, indeed, and I can anticipate what those bits of information might be. As to the matter of the settlement between Miss Wembley and the writing team of Mr.

Favell and Miss Wentworth, this was a strictly confidential matter and I was not at liberty to discuss it, in fact, none of the principals are – or I should say were – allowed to discuss the terms. Miss Wembley's unfortunate demise did not change that. However, your recent discovery has upset those considerations a bit."

Miss Francis's eyes grew larger with each passing sentence which he spoke, and she didn't hide her displeasure that Tumworth seemed to anticipate her every move and her next questions. "But you could have at least told me there was a connection between Miss Wembley and the would-be writing team, instead of sending me scurrying in Mr. Doveless's direction for something that had no substance. And, by the way, as for the new book itself, I have sources that confirm there's nothing the slightest bit scandalous in it. I dare say another of your red herrings, Mr. Tumworth."

A mildly admonishing index finger from Tumworth, then, "Please ... Harrison, if you will. Yes, that all was a bit malicious on my part, wasn't it, but then again, misdirection in the legal world is a fair technique; someday you'll understand these things." He didn't hide the tone of condescension in his voice.

The color in Miss Francis's face was turning a mild shade of pink and her breathing became a little faster. "Believe me, Mr. Tumworth, or Mr. Harrison, or whatever you wish to be called, I'm only too familiar with legal maneuverings and do not approve of your tactics, much less your tired explanations. These types of antics I'd expect from someone of Mr. Thrugg's ilk, but not a gentleman of your stature."

Ignoring her little dig, Tumworth's gentle response was in the form of a compliment. "Yes, I'm well aware that you're versed in legal goings on, negotiations and such; your reputation is well-known. But I must say, Miss Francis, you've certainly gotten yourself most exercised over all this." He poured himself a drink, with due thoroughness in his usual leisurely manner. "Are you sure you won't join me, a little libation, to calm the nerves."

A rapid shake of the head in the negative.

"Well, chin-chin." He put the glass to his mouth and took small swig. "Anyhow, yes, I'll admit what I gave you did not produce the best results, but who can ever predict what an ace detective such as yourself might turn up, with even the slimmest of material to go on? As to the money being deposited in Miss Niffin's bank account – "

"How did you know I was going to ask about this?"

A mild breath of impatience. "My dear Miss Francis, it's my job to anticipate these things, and you forget, I have sources, too, which serves to refresh my recollection. Please permit me to give credit where credit is due, and to offer my compliments for the fine work done by your private detective or whomever else you might have engaged to work for you. Quite a nice bit of digging and uncovering." He lifted his glass in a toast.

"Thanks."

"By the way, word has gotten around you were seen strolling the malecón with a certain famous personage. Is it possible he's involved in your investigations somehow?"

Just as she'd expected, he knew not only what she'd found out but who was assisting her as well. Moreover, he seemed to know the exact points she was going to challenge him on. But she wasn't going to give him any satisfaction. "A proverbial no comment, sir, but what about Miss Niffin? The money deposited certainly wasn't just for her salary."

"That is correct. Her salary is exactly forty eight dollars a week, not in your league, not even in Miss Wembley's league, far from it, but pretty respectable money for a personal secretary. In any event the extra thousand a month was some sort of bonus, for what reason I cannot tell you, simply because I do not know. Whether Miss Wembley was fond of the woman or if there was blackmail involved, or whatever the considerations were, I have no information. My instructions were to set up a special account – we called it a foundation of sorts – to obscure exactly what was being done, I'm sure you can understand the need to be discreet. In any event, I was the only person who had access to said account and I was to withdraw one thousand dollars per month and deposit the money into Miss Niffin's account, no questions asked. That was the extent of my knowledge. I never got to know Miss Niffin personally, only met her a couple of times in the ten years or so she worked for Miss Wembley."

Miss Francis was listening intently. "It all seems extremely irregular – and very suspicious. Anyway I'm developing some ideas of my own, and it all sort of fits together, and no, I'm not going to tell you what my ideas are." She was delighted just this once she could administer Tumworth a proverbial dose of his own medicine. "That serves to remind me, please join the rest of us in the main ballroom at eight o'clock tomorrow night; all the writerly principals and myself are having a little soirée, in which I'll try to sort out the recent events."

Again the oily smile. "The gathering of the suspects, and the unmasking of the murderer. How exciting. I must say, Miss Francis, you do have your detective methodology down pat."

"Thanks. But, continuing with the gathering of suspects idea, permit me a question, if I may?

"By all means."

She continued, "As regards the suspects, and in confidence, what is your strictly expert professional opinion as to who might have – "

He held up his right hand in one of his patented protective gestures and said, "Now Miss Francis, you should know my role is to defend someone once he's been accused, not to try to find out who done it; that's your department. Thus you'll excuse me if I take a pass on your question, however tempted I am to offer an opinion in consideration of your understandable curiosity."

"Have it your way. But now I must go. Don't forget, eight o'clock tomorrow."

He responded only with one of his enigmatic smiles and a barely perceptible nod.

CHAPTER 9

By now it was late afternoon, and she sufficed with a light dinner at a nearby cocina, afterwards sneaking back to her suite and settling in for an early evening. All the sleuthing was beginning to exhaust her, but she was restless. She struggled with her encounter with Mr. Tumworth earlier in the day. Why did he conceal those important bits of information from her? Did he have his own reasons for doing so? Client confidentiality or no, this was a capital case after all.

She wrote a few sentences in her diary, and after reading for a bit her mind eventually calmed down and she sank into a delicious sleep and woke up once and drifted back into sleep's comforting refuge. She dreamed, first of Mazatlán's imagery: the lapping waves, colonial arches, red tile roofs and warm breezes which soothed her sweating forehead. But halfway into the night her images took a turn. She was lying on her back in some indeterminate place, and a girl with a vaguely languorous look on her face was bent over her. The girl was garbed in a sheer nightgown, and there was a full-figuredness about her that Miss Francis's imagination found both exciting and dangerous. She could see the girl's dark brown eyes and orchid-in-the-moonlight skin as she moved closer, closer until she felt the warm, moist breath on her skin. Miss Francis closed her eyes in a delicious anticipation; her back arched and she awaited the warm lips to kiss her. She felt, and heard, her heart beating, as well as a faint sound of pounding, like a thumping, from an unknown source. But just then the girl took out a knife and began pull it back behind her shoulder, high beyond her head as if about to strike …

Again the thumping from some uncertain direction. She drifted back to a half sleep but the figure of the girl transmogrified itself into what looked like John Barrymore. The images were of Barrymore creeping up silently, guilty-like, as if ready to use the knife, or was it a gun he had? Or perhaps he was about to strangle her. Then the tableaux changed again – it wasn't she but Miss Wembley who was the stalked prey. The figure of Barrymore then metamorphosed into the colorful Mr. Portifoy, the self-proclaimed murderer. Just as fast the images of the man and Barrymore blended into one figure and disappeared. Then the loud thumping noises. Gunshots? Were they part of the dream or not?

The noises continued as she awoke with a jolt and exclaimed triumphantly, *That's it! I've got it.*

She looked around, dazed and not quite awake, trying to move in bed. She turned on the light, then drew her hand across her forehead, brushing away the loose strands of hair, then she pushed back the gossamer silk sheets which covered her. She stumbled to the bathroom, put on her satin nightgown and felt more or less able to receive the company at the door.

But then she remembered, what was it she said? *I've got it.* What did it mean?

The pounding at the door, louder & more insistent. *"Señorita Francis! Está bien? Por favor, abre la puerta."*

She walked across the cold, tiled floor and let in two men who were dressed in hotel staff uniforms. She recognized one as being the night man from the other evening, and he said with open palms, "Many thousand regrets but a matter, needs you, at police station."

A long breath. "Is the matter so urgent it needs me at three o'clock in the morning? Can't it wait?"

"Most assure you, not to bother at unkind hour, *si no necessario*. we would not be disturb you at such sad time. A most, how you say, delicacy situation. They say to bring lots of cash."

"Who are *they*? Oh, never mind. Give me a few minutes to put on some clothes and I'll meet you downstairs in the lobby."

Ten minutes later she walked into the lobby. She withdrew a generous amount of cash from the hotel safe at the desk, and she was ready to go. The policeman there to greet her escorted her into an official vehicle and they drove down to the police station. The officer didn't say anything while they were on the way; she sensed he was nervous and uncomfortable in his role. They entered the building and the man led her through the front offices back to the jail cells area.

While they were walking she said, "Where's Captain Seguro?"

"Sorry, Captain is away, in Tepic, a case, but return tomorrow."

A sigh. "I suppose that will have to do. But it's good he's returning tomorrow; there may be developments in our case here." The officer said nothing.

They arrived at the farthest cell on the left, and she could hardly believe what she saw. There, locked up, was Errol Flynn, along with the director John Ford and an up and coming actor she recognized. She knew him as John Wayne. There was also a scruffy looking young man she didn't recognize. They were all shabbily dressed in some sort of sailor's clothes, and their hair was mussed. Flynn and Ford had bruises on their faces. They all looked dirty and tired and she could smell the fusty odor of alcohol as it drifted through the cell.

The policeman unlocked the cell door and allowed her to go in as he hovered nearby with a second officer in close watch.

Flynn managed a tired smile. It seemed as though he had been designated as spokesman for the other three. "Kay, dearest, I knew you'd come through for us." He made a gesture with his hand in the direction of his three comrades. "I'm sure you know Mr. Ford and Mr. Wayne, and this is one of my yacht stewards, Johnny West." The three men said nothing, rather looking like whipped dogs as they held their heads down in what seemed a combination of embarrassment and exhaustion.

A nod from Miss Francis. "Much pleasure, Mr. West." Then her attention returned to Flynn. "Now Errol, would you mind telling me what this is about, something so important to wake me in the middle of the night."

"Let me say we're so glad to see you here, and many, many apologies, Kay darling, but I knew with your generous nature you'd understand."

"Understand what? Come on, man, get to it."

Flynn sneaked a glance at Ford and Wayne, as if entreating support. "Well, it's a little complicated, but the gist is that … you see, we got into an altercation at a certain local establishment."

She cocked her head in a skeptical pose. "What kind of altercation? What establishment?"

"It's a truly high class, uh, in its way, business, named the Hotel Blue. It's located in a part of town where the lights are more … red-colored, if you get my drift." Then the entreating smile. "Perhaps you've heard of it."

She rolled her eyes, "No, I'm afraid not. But you don't have to sugar coat it; I get your message. You're a man of the world and all that."

Flynn merely responded with open palms. "Whatever you say, dear Kay."

"Right now I say go on with your story."

"Well, anyway, we were sitting at the bar attached to the … hotel, having some libations, minding our own business, listening to the talented mariachi musicians – that's why we went there, we'd heard great things about the music."

She groaned and rolled her eyes once more.

Flynn continued, "Then, wouldn't you know it, these charming young ladies came over to our table, joined us, and we were all having a gay old time, enjoying the wine, each other's company, and the wonderful music. But before we knew it these four Mexican thugs appeared and verbally attacked us, casting vile aspersions upon these nice ladies, in most distasteful fashion, I assure you. Such an insult, these sweet girls. These louts had a few choice comments for us too. Well, it was something we just couldn't let stand."

"And you had to come to the defense of the ladies' honor."

"That's about it," Flynn said, a lilt in his voice as he smiled hopefully.

"Well? Go on, and get to the point, for goodness sake."

"Well, as you say, we had to defend the honor of the ladies and the argument got a little physical and – needless to say we mopped the floor with these characters – but in the process did a little damage to the fine establishment."

"How much damage?"

"Well, for some reason the police were called in, and when things were sorted out they said we'd have to pay for the property damages and ... court costs." A glance at the two officers and a hint of a wink to Miss Francis. "As it happens we're all a little short on local legal tender. And not only that, we needed someone of standing to vouch for us, to properly spring us from jail – that reminds me, there's the fees to post bail, too – and then we'd have to agree to leave town right away." Again the imploring grin. "Of course I immediately thought of you as a person of unimpeachable integrity – the confidence the local authorities have placed in you, practically an official of the Mexican government. Anyway, these fine officers assure me if costs are paid and we are vouched for, they'll forgive everything. And that's my story, my dearest Kay. In short, my colleagues and myself throw ourselves upon your most generous mercy."

"Don't overdo it." She shook her head back and forth in a disapproving manner. "Oh, Errol, Errol, I come to expect this type of behavior from you. I can't speak for Mr. Wayne or Mr. West, but Mr. Ford, really, I'm surprised, a man of your caliber getting mixed up in something like this." Ford said nothing, and she returned her gaze to Flynn. "Anyway, what's the amount?"

Another glance by Flynn in Ford's direction. Then Flynn muttered in a soft voice, "Five thousand pesos." His eyes squinted and his shoulders hunched up as he said the words.

"Five thousand pesos! Good Lord, what on earth do you think? That I'm made of money?"

"You've got to understand, dearest, it's not only costs for property damage and the court fees." Another glance at the policemen. "But the traditional forgiveness costs down here that, well, bring up the price."

Another shaking of the head, only this time slower and heavier. "Oh, Errol, Errol." A look away and a long breath of disgust. "Never mind."

She reached into her handbag, took out a roll of bills, counted out five thousand pesos and handed it to the more senior officer. "Here."

The officer took the money, tipped his cap and smiled broadly. "*Muy amable. Muchas gracias, señorita.*"

She then turned to Flynn. "Lucky you I was tipped off to bring lots of cash. Well, congratulations, Errol, you've ruined a good night's sleep and also cost me a considerable amount of money in the process."

"But Kay, think of it this way: you've done a good deed for your fellow man, and I'm sure that makes you feel better."

"What makes me feel better is I get a little benefit out of this comedy, namely, this will square us for all the assistance you've provided me lately. Anyway, I'm going back to the hotel and try to get some rest, and you and your friends will promise me to be off in a hurry."

With the familiar gesture of the open palms, Flynn said, "Kay dearest, we are eternally in your debt. And, if you'll indulge me, there's one more little thing ... "

"You try my patience, Errol. Oh, all right, what might that little thing be?"

"To be precise, can I rely on your discretion in this matter? Lili doesn't exactly approve of such diversions, and if the press ever got hold of this, we'd never hear the end of it."

Another long sigh. "Yes, you can rely on my ... discretion. Now, if you'll excuse me I intend to get back to the hotel and try to get some rest; tomorrow will be a big day, and by the way, I'll fill you in on how everything works out."

"Much appreciated. As always, you're a darling."

With Miss Francis in close pursuit, Flynn and the others made their way out of the building quickly. Once outside they said their goodbyes, and the four men veritably tip toed away in the direction of the wharf. She only looked at them shaking her head, barely suppressing a smile.

She walked back to the hotel, again finding herself taking the route along the malecón which hugged Olas Altas Drive. It was a couple of hours before sunrise, and the night was vintage Mazatlán: a gentle breeze with a hint of wind-borne jungle scents and plenty of moon, the foamy breakers down below, and fishing craft twinkling out at sea. Except for some faint music from the harbor boats, the town was quiet as though gently covered with a thick coating of warm milk. She liked things that way; she could think, and thinking was what she needed to do. She stopped for a while to sit, and noticed the boats gliding gently over the water, the moon on its silent journey to the dark horizon, and the breeze bearing fragrances of wildflowers and a faint scent of salt from the ocean. A calm wrapped itself around the city, but Miss Francis's psyche was restless as she struggled with the puzzle of the murder; she was almost there but lacked just one more piece, one more key, if only she could find it.

CHAPTER 10

The hotel's main ballroom was located on the ground floor in the back, just beyond the open air lobby. At its furthest expanse it spilled out into the lush tropical gardens. But tonight the ballroom was empty; only the great chandelier dominated the interior. Miss Francis had instructed the hotel staff to arrange chairs on the stage where the band usually played, to be situated in most theatrical, semi-circular fashion. She knew how to stage an event, and made sure in this case she was going to be the star performer.

All the interested parties were there, even the ebullient Johnny Caballero, who had been recalled for the denouement to add support and even a little more force if necessary. Though in truth Johnny was just window dressing, since Captain Seguro was also present, waiting in the wings, as it were, peering near a side door which gave him a perfect view of all the goings on. As for the principals, Miss Wentworth and

Mr. Favell looked confident in their well tended, smart attire, but nonetheless they couldn't hide their considerable nervousness, their eyes darting around restlessly as they fidgeted in the less than comfortable chairs. Mr. Tumworth was present, in über-British glory, wearing a light grey herringbone suit which must have been impossibly hot and uncomfortable, even in the late autumn's friendlier temperatures. He was studiously perusing a copy of the *California Law Review*, seemingly oblivious to the events unfolding around him. As for the ever low-keyed Miss Niffin, she chose the chair most distant from the middle; she must have thought it would allow her to slip away unnoticed in her patented invisible manner. Buck LaRue, Claire Luckingham and Percy Doveless rounded out the proceedings.

Befitting the semi-official nature of the event Miss Francis wanted to make a favorable impression, and accordingly wore a rather understated, tight fitting dark gray business suit of exceptional tailoring that came down to her ankles. She supplemented the suit with a rounded, curvy, small hat and black Rinsetta shoes. To the elegant clothes she added only a modest assortment of jewelry: an emerald brooch, matching emerald bracelet and one ruby ring on her little finger.

Finally Miss Francis got up and began to speak.

"I requested you all come here tonight so we might look at the various aspects of Miss Wembley's unfortunate demise, and determine conclusively who the murderer is." She spoke with her clear, ringing tone, befitting her status as a veteran of the stage as well as the cinema.

"Oh, and by the way, not only is Captain Seguro

present, but he's posted two of his men at each entrance to the ballroom and four additional men outside the hotel's main entrance, so please don't give any thought to trying to escape." She glanced in the Captain's direction. "And while I'm on the matter of Captain Seguro, your man who followed me to the church and through half the town, he's no doubt here tonight too. And believe me when I say I'm touched by your solicitude."

The Captain tipped his hat ever so slightly and motioned to a little man on the other side of the ballroom to show himself. He had been hiding behind yet another of the strategically placed palms. Captain Seguro said, "Miss Francis, may I more or less formally present to you Lt. Gomez." The little man stepped forward and touched his fingers to his forehead, then flicked them in her direction in a mild gesture of respect and acknowledgment.

Miss Francis smiled and nodded to Lt. Gomez, then paused a moment for emphasis. Then she walked over to where Percy Doveless was sitting. She stood to the side of him and put her hand benevolently on his shoulder.

She then stepped back and said, "But getting back to the matter at hand, we begin with Percy, a most unlikely suspect."

Listening intently, Percy brushed off her comment with an indulgent shrug and a breezy wave of the hand.

"Rumor had it Mr. Percy Doveless, critic extraordinaire and all around *bon vivant*, might take umbrage as to what was in the pages of Miss Wembley's soon to be released novel, *The Long Lavender Goodbye*. With such a title, how could one not be curious? But rest assured, through discussions with Percy and private detective-cum-book critic Johnny Caballero, I've assured myself there wasn't anything in the new novel to offend Percy, or to offend anyone in particular for that matter. But – Percy had other secrets to protect."

Catherine Wentworth leaned over toward Jack Favell and whispered something to him. They both indulged themselves in a private chuckle while glancing in Percy's direction.

And of course their little distraction caught Miss Francis's eagle eye. Percy only smiled all the while as if entertained by their antics, perhaps even a little flattered, but Miss Francis was clearly not amused.

"I interrupt my analysis to direct your attention to Mr. Favell and Miss Wentworth, who find something I just said or am about to say incredibly humorous. I'm afraid I'll have to disappoint them; really, such sophomoric attempts at levity."

Their response was to just sit there unsmiling, Miss Wentworth's visage metamorphosing into a glower as she stared at Miss Francis.

"Anyhow, as I was saying – Percy had other matters to be discreet about. You see, it seems Percy was taking private writing lessons with the great lady, and please excuse me for rather unchivalrously exposing this little secret of his. I only bring it up because it's germane to the rest of the story and helps to unmask our killer. Percy was not alone in hoping some of Miss Wembley's greatness would rub off on him, but as far as we know he's the only one who formally studied with her. Alas, he probably found out early on she wasn't much of a teacher and not very enlightening as to the mystery writer's art, and indeed there's a reason for this … but I get ahead of myself. In any case this explains his discontinuing studying with her after only a few lessons."

While she was talking Percy smiled and shook his head slowly in concurrence.

Miss Francis then strolled over to Claire Luckingham's chair. "Another possible candidate, less easily dispensed with, is Miss Luckingham, a most interesting and highly ambitious lady. She has two strikes against her. First, she certainly stood to benefit from Miss Wembley's demise – the new queen of mystery writers and all that. Then there's the spat she and Miss Wembley had, so visible at the restaurant, more genuine than manufactured, to my way of thinking." Miss Luckingham's body arched backwards as if in a defensive mode, and she moved her head slowly in Miss Francis's direction,

Miss Francis continued with a reassuring lifting of her right hand. "But it's all right, Miss L; I accept your version of the events, however less spicy they may be. But more to the point, you couldn't have been the killer; your, shall we say, persona, doesn't quite fit. I'll elaborate later."

"But now I would like to talk about the late, and not so lamented, Mr. Henry Thrugg, a suspect in absentia, and whom it would be neglectful to the point of insult for me to leave out. He was sensitive about those things, you know. In any case, would it be more accurate for me to refer to him as Mr. Jock O'Halloran? That's the closest we've gotten to a real name. For now we'll call him Mr. Thrugg for simplicity's sake. He was definitely involved but not wasn't the perpetrator of the crime. No, it seems Mr. Thrugg is guilty of two, related, to be sure, and crucial, but somewhat more tangential crimes.

"First, he is obviously responsible for Miss Wembley taking ill so conveniently at the last moment; he slipped her some sort of Mickey Finn, probably a low grade poison to simulate sickness and influenza-like symptoms. His other, more colorful contribution was the hiring, or to be more precise, being the middle man, in obtaining the services of the two local ruffians, who in turn transported the body, miraculously undetected, up the stairs to my suite. It's still not exactly clear as to the purpose of such an eccentric tactic, perhaps to frame me for the crime, a diversion to distract attention, or perhaps to frame the two unfortunate dupes who were tempted by the five hundred peso fee for a few minutes' work.

"In either case Mr. Thrugg was the man in the middle, caught in a web, tantalized with a large sum of money or blackmailed with the threat of exposure to the authorities, ultimately lured to the beach and shot so brutally and ruthlessly three times at close range by the same gun that shot and killed Miss Wembley."

Miss Francis was in her element. She lorded over the proceedings as if it was second nature to her, and it probably was, like one of her dinner parties in which she famously held court with haughty aplomb. She walked slowly, measuredly, then stopped and stood just behind where Jack Favell and Catherine Wentworth were sitting. Their stiff posture suggested they were none too happy with her nearby presence.

"Now we consider the case of Mr. Favell and Miss Wentworth. They've been a bit naughty, they have, leaving out as they did quite an important part of their history with Miss Wembley. I was left to patch it together using various sources. It seems they came to their own accommodation with the lady, but that was settled long ago, and I won't be so insensitive as to go into the details but rather, simply pose the question: they were here for a reason, and what was the reason? I don't think we could call them fans of hers, and they weren't here for writing instruction or any other type of literary inspiration. Were they planning to shake her down further?"

A raised hand of assurance by Miss Francis. "No need to explain. And yet – one is tempted to infer their purpose was something even more nefarious, inspired by overwhelming malice and spite, compounded by Miss Wembley's conspicuous success as an author. If so, our authentic murderer beat them to the punch, just better and faster. But alas, there are no laws on the books for crimes merely contemplated and which remain uncommitted; were that the case how many of us in this room would be totally guiltless?"

Miss Wentworth leapt up from her chair, her face contorted as she said in a loud, shaking voice, "I'll have you know we won't stand for this! We've had just about enough of these amateur theatrics from this frumped-up, has-been actress turned know-it-all detective. I for one will not sit here any more and listen to these slanderous accusations. Jack?"

"Cathy, darling," he said as he got up from his chair and clasped her hand. They started to walk out of the ballroom and two of Captain Seguro's men walked in their direction as if to try to stop them.

Miss Francis waved them off and said, "Let them go; it's been a difficult week, especially for her, and whatever their other transgressions, they aren't the guilty parties here." Captain Seguro did not interfere, merely nodding to his men in concurrence with Miss Francis.

Miss Francis then continued, "All the same, we *are* running out of suspects."

She gave a look in the direction of Mr. Tumworth, then strolled over towards him, her shoes creating an echo effect in the large room with every step.

"Speaking of things like guilt and innocence, we now consider Mr. Tumworth, he who says so much but reveals so little. To begin, let us dismiss any culpability of Mr. Tumworth. No, his crime is the very legal practice of assassination by pen and paper, not with guns. But he did have his secrets and was the victim of a cruel bit of fate. No, he was not in any danger of imminent dismissal as Miss Wembley's lawyer, though this had been intimated by the ever unreliable Mr. Thrugg.

"As for the dramatic, seemingly mysterious death of Mr. Tumworth's legal colleague, Mr. Craig, some expert detective work by Captain Seguro and his staff resulted in a decidedly sensible explanation. You see, unknown to Mr. Tumworth, and the rest of us for that matter, Mr. Craig suffered from a peanut allergy; even the slightest intake of a peanut-related product would result in a violent reaction, possibly even death, which did indeed occur. It seems the restaurant chefs, through no fault of their own, used a rare peanut oil in preparing one of the Chinese dishes which Mr. Craig in most untimely fashion had the misfortune to order. Thus his violent manner of death inspired all sorts of wild, conspiratorial inferences, temporarily reviving the idea there was something in Miss Wembley's new book so scandalous someone was willing to exact as revenge the act of murder itself. This can all now be explained away in rather more pedestrian fashion."

Then a walk in the direction of Buck LaRue. "As for Mr. LaRue, he is the least likely person to have done the deed, and unlike fictional mysteries, he is not our actual murderer. Indeed, Mr. LaRue was never a genuine suspect – too honest a face, amongst other qualities. But more to the point, as a writer of formulaic Westerns Mr. LaRue simply didn't have the imagination to concoct such a complex and ingenious scheme as the murder of Miss Wembley and its subsequent cover-up. For something this subtle we have to look elsewhere, to someone with a first-class intellect and indeed a mystery writer's touch. But nonetheless Mr. LaRue provided one of the best clues which clearly established a connection between Mr. Thrugg and the murderer, whom we'll get to momentarily."

She walked over to the farthest chair, in the direction of Miss Niffin.

"Finally we consider Miss Niffin, dedicated, ever loyal and self-effacing secretary and confidant to the great lady. Alas, her visit to Mazatlán with her employer was to turn out to be a fateful, even tragic, holiday in ways she never expected, a case of literally getting a lot more than she bargained for, and most dramatically so."

Up to now Miss Niffin had been sitting calmly, but her body tensed, her eyes widened and her pallor grew a little paler with each of Miss Francis's passing sentences.

Miss Francis walked to the center of the chairs and paused for a moment. Then she said, "But I'm afraid we must back up a bit, to about a week or so ago, just before she and her mistress came down to Mazatlán. They were overheard arguing with raised voices, the exact contents of the discussion being uncertain – the witness was a maid who has limited facility with English – but one of the voices said she deserved more in the circumstances, and the other voice saying she's been especially generous, or something to that effect.

"There is the obvious problem of which voice said what, but no matter. The content of their conversation suggests a simple explanation: Miss Niffin learns Miss Wembley is about to change her will, presumably to Miss Niffin's disfavor, and, in a fit of rage, kills her employer, thus protecting her bequest. It's a logical and classic motive for murder, but in our case the wrong motive. No, the motive lay elsewhere, and the fact that Miss Wembley was about to change the will where Miss Niffin would now inherit the great bulk of the legacy is now rendered irrelevant.

"But all this we'll elaborate in due course. Let us now return to the fateful evening. As mentioned before, it's obvious now Mr. Thrugg slipped some kind of poison into Miss Wembley's drink that night around seven o'clock, thus her seeming illness and inability to attend *The Letter* at the theatre. And this is where things get ... interesting.

"First, there's the rather bland note of regret delivered to Somerset Maugham, supposedly written by Miss Wembley or dictated by her to Miss Niffin, but with a few revealing errors which were noticed right away by Mr. Maugham himself. This is all curious and not easily explained, though hardly conclusive proof in itself. Then we have the problem of all the principal suspects being present at the theatre and afterward at the restaurant. It seems none of them could have been back at the hotel to commit the murder while at the same time being at these places as well. A person can't be in two places at once – or can she? I do use the word she, because it's at this point, or more precisely, just a little earlier, that we have an amazing identity transformation, or to be more precise still, impersonation, which occurred, probably during interval at the theatre. But first, let us digress just a bit.

"You see, most of you have probably heard there was a B actress in town named Leah Lavish, whose body, it would seem, was discovered over in the Juarez District, brutally murdered only a few hours after Miss Wembley's unfortunate demise. Could there be a connection between the two murders? The preliminary opinion was no, there was not. But further examination reveals there is indeed a connection between the two murders. And this brings us to a second transformation, at the very place of the murder of the unfortunate Miss Lavish. The significance, and the resulting, indeed inevitable solution to all three murders, is this: the sad events of the past few days are the work of not one, but two killers, and improbable as it may seem, our recently deceased Miss Lavish is very much alive."

Miss Francis paused, then looked at 'Miss Niffin', and said, "Aren't you, Miss Lavish?"

All the guests let out collective, muffled gasps. 'Miss Niffin' returned Miss Francis's gaze with a cold stare and said, "You tell a pretty good story, and I am entertained. Please continue."

"I will, though it gives me no pleasure to do so. But to return to Miss Niffin: she was an excellent researcher, possessing a Master's degree cum laude from a fine East Coast school, and moreover, she had substantial means which gave her access to sources like private investigators. Miss Niffin found out about Miss Lavish's, shall we say colorful background, which included work as an actress, mime, magician, and crucially, impersonator, but even more important, knowledge of her criminal record, one of the crimes being accessory to murder. Miss Niffin probably put it to Miss Lavish there was some sort of practical joke going on, and she, Miss Niffin, would pay handsomely to have Miss Lavish impersonate her for just a few hours at the opera. Thus, Miss Lavish was brought here for a specific acting role.

"The first borrowing of identity occurred probably during the intermission. While the real Miss Niffin slipped away to do the terrible deed, Miss Lavish was by now impersonating her brilliantly, a little too much so in fact, overplaying her hand by talking conspicuously with a dazzling blonde in the foyer, a woman she probably didn't even know, just to underscore her presence at the theatre but somewhat at odds with Miss Niffin's shy, retiring personality. This slip notwithstanding, there was little chance the others would recognize she wasn't the real Miss Niffin; Miss Lavish was expert at disguising herself and curiously already bore a resemblance to Miss Niffin. Moreover, in her low-keyed role over the years Miss Niffin had been practically invisible; even Mr. Tumworth hadn't seen her more than two times in ten years."

Tumworth interrupted the monologue with his usual ponderous insightfulness and oily delivery. "This is all very fascinating, but assuming this fantastical tale has any accuracy, where's the motive? You've as much said it wasn't the will. People don't go around committing murder just as some sort of practical joke."

Miss Francis nodded thoughtfully, and couldn't help wondering whether he was already honing his skills as defense attorney for 'Miss Niffin'.

She continued, "Indeed they do not, which bring us to question of motive. As Mr. Tumworth implies, albeit rather circuitously, the motive wasn't profit, since Miss Wembley had been depositing one thousand dollars a month into Miss Niffin's bank account for several years."

All the remaining persons of interest looked at each other with incredulous stares. Then Mr. Tumworth offered, "Why then, pray tell, kill the goose that laid the golden egg? It makes no sense."

"Why indeed? But if you'll bear with me just a bit more we'll get to that."

At this moment Mr. Tumworth rather unchivalrously continued with his protestations. "But assuming, and just assuming for sake of argument, that your highly imaginative tale has any merit, how the devil could Miss Niffin have crept back into the hotel, done the murder, and crept back out of the hotel, in front of all the guests in the lobby and the bar, without being seen in plain view?" He was in best lawyerly form as he probed for any weaknesses in Miss Francis's scenario of the events, his vanilla coated voice assuming a sharper edge as he spoke.

But she wasn't flustered as she seemed to anticipate his skepticism. "Mr. Tumworth makes an excellent point, but the explanation is actually quite simple. As we've now established, the formidable Mr. Thrugg was in confederacy with Miss Niffin and doubtless had knowledge of the hotel; it would be a simple matter for him to find a clandestine way in and out of the building. No, nothing so melodramatic as a secret passage but merely knowing the right set of obscure stairs to take to remain undetected."

With a look almost too eager, Mr. Tumworth pounced again. "But you forget the little detail about the blast from the gunshots. Surely someone would have heard such a commotion."

A smile from Miss Francis. "No doubt the same thought occurred to our killer, who took appropriate precautions in the form of a silencer, perhaps, or in any case was able to muffle the sound in some way as to avoid detection. And with the music and voices from the hotel bar and the street noise on a Saturday night, such a precaution would almost be unnecessary, but you can be sure our murderer had some sort of insurance plan just in case, and in the end the strategy worked; all the guests in nearby rooms and the lobby who were interviewed reported hearing nothing out of the ordinary."

Mr. Tumworth sighed deeply and nodded. "Advantage to you, Miss Francis – for now."

She continued, "To return to the events of the fateful evening: the part about moving the body was orchestrated by the real Miss Niffin to throw suspicion on the two ruffians, or perhaps suggest Mr. Thrugg, a natural suspect, was the real murderer. But somewhere in the late evening, Miss Lavish, no stranger to criminal enterprises, had figured out *she* was probably the next victim, and concocts – or improvises – the plan to kill Miss Niffin, and to continue impersonating her, for however long she can get away with it, then if necessary, simply disappear and re-emerge elsewhere under a new identity, in the process eliminating a witness to her involvement in this crime.

"Miss Lavish probably already had her suspicions – by now she knew Miss Wembley had mysteriously taken ill – and when Miss Niffin suggested they meet in an out the way district in town, presumably for Miss Lavish to receive payment for her acting services, she sensed something malodorous about whole affair, and she was right. No doubt Miss Niffin planned to shoot her with the same gun and remove a troublesome and potentially complicating accomplice to *her* scheme, but she hadn't realized Miss Lavish had the same idea, only did it better. So Miss Lavish awaited her or perhaps followed her and delivered the *coup de gras* with a blow to the head, several blows to the head, with a blunt object, a metal pipe or club perhaps.

"It was probably at this time, to be exact, she conceives the idea she and Miss Niffin could exchange identities on a more permanent basis, a clever plan actually; the physical resemblance was there and she already proved she could pose as Miss Niffin around the very people who should know who she was, so she exchanged her clothes and identity papers with Miss Niffin, and even took Miss Niffin's gun, which she later used to dispatch the unfortunate Mr. Thrugg, and ... *voilà*. The dead girl in the Juarez barrio was a minor actress named Leah Lavish, who was visiting Mazatlán for her own private reasons, and wandered into a dubious district, met her sad fate and is soon forgotten, a classic case of the authorities – and myself – being so preoccupied with finding the murderer that we didn't pay sufficient attention to the true identity of the victim, who in reality was the unfortunate Miss Niffin.

"But to get back to Miss Lavish, the real one, not the presumed dead one, she realized she'd need to get rid of the troublesome Mr. Thrugg, who had been badgering her over payment of the funds which – unknown to her – had been promised him, threatening her with exposure or worse.

"As to the obvious question of why didn't Miss Lavish simply leave town after the murder, instead of attempting something so cumbersome and risky as exchanging places with Miss Niffin, well, where could she go? Officially she was now dead and the impending disappearance of Miss Niffin would have looked most suspicious and inspired more investigation, resulting in her inevitable exposure and status of fugitive. So in her mind it was a good choice simply to assume the identity of Miss Niffin, play along and quietly slip out of town. And the challenge of pulling it off probably appealed to her actor's vanity, thus far cruelly frustrated by her lack of success in the film industry. But – she didn't count on two things: the persistence of Mr. Thrugg, and her own tell-tale mistakes which would ultimately give her away."

Still unconvinced, Mr. Tumworth attempted to interject himself one more time. "For the moment, accepting your thesis, then please answer a very basic question: why didn't Miss Niffin simply pay off Miss Lavish; wouldn't it have been cleaner and less dangerous?"

"Another good point. We can't know Miss Niffin's emotional state at the time, much less her logic; we can only infer from the facts as we know them. No, there's no absolute evidence Miss Niffin went to meet Miss

Lavish in the Juarez district with the plan of murdering her, but the details suggest at the very least she took the gun with her.

"Yes, Miss Niffin could have left the gun in her hotel room and Miss Lavish could have retrieved later, but to leave a murder weapon in one's own hotel suite, so incriminating, not likely. It's also possible that indeed it was her intention to pay off Miss Lavish all along, and she was merely taking the gun with her as protection in a rough district. In any case what happened next … we are uncertain. An argument, perhaps, or Miss Lavish awaited her in ambush, but however the events transpired, this is where Miss Niffin's untimely demise occurred. Certainly Miss Lavish wouldn't have killed her somewhere else and moved the body there. Perhaps further light will be shed on the details through conversation with Miss Lavish.

"As for the ultimate disposition of the murder weapon we can only assume the gun has been discarded, probably in the ocean after the dispatching of the unfortunate Mr. Thrugg."

Mr. Tumworth sighed deeply and nodded. "You win this set, Miss Francis."

Miss Francis acknowledged the compliment with a simple, curt "Thank you," her rather proud bearing suggesting she was pleased with herself that she had beaten the great man at his own legalistic game.

A pause by Miss Francis, and some slow nodding and a hint of a smile. "A good plan, well carried out, brilliant in certain ways. Miss Lavish might have gotten away with it, for a while anyway, but – there were a couple of revealing mistakes, understandable insofar as hers were crimes more of panic, and improvisation, than profit or passion. For all we know her actions were self-defense. Are you listening, Mr. Tumworth?"

"In any event, and self-defense or no, when she took on the identity of Miss Niffin, the actress Leah Lavish was at the very least participating in a serious obstruction of justice. And then there was the more cold-blooded murder of Mr. Thrugg. But as to the mistakes, first there's the detail of the fingerprints on the wine glass which she drank from when speaking to me. Captain Seguro and his American colleagues will be able to verify they are indeed the prints of Leah Lavish and not Miss Niffin, and please, don't try to deny it, Miss Lavish. Then there were two more revealing slips, appropriately of a literary nature, that Miss Lavish committed. First was her formal report to the authorities, she now being disguised as Miss Niffin. This report was written in an unpolished style by one of limited language skills, at odds with the real Miss Niffin's penchant for flowery, poetic prose.

"Then there was the little tell when she described Miss Wembley's fans as 'legionary' when she meant to say 'legion.' The real Miss Niffin, with her elegant education, would never make such a mistake.

"There was also the matter of Miss Lavish's flat Middle Western accent which kept creeping into her speech, although she did her best to camouflage it and speak in Miss Niffin's more genteel Ivy League delivery, and did a reasonably good job with her considerable acting and impersonation skills. She also did well playing the grieving employee and intimate, but, as was her tendency, she rather overplayed – or in this case underplayed – the role, speaking in a whispery voice and all the while coughing and looking down or away when talking to me, as if trying to hide her features. There was something about her affected manner that suggested more than just pathological shyness and grief.

"But now we must leave Miss Lavish and get back to Mr. Tumworth's protestations of motive as it applies to the first crime, Miss Wembley's demise, carried out by the real Miss Niffin. For all its planning and analytic detail, this was ultimately a crime of passion. Let us return to the Mexican maid, who speaks little English. She overhears raised voices and some words, not conclusive, but quite incriminating in their way. But we have misinterpreted the substance of the conversation by assuming it had something to do with the will. Even if it did have something to do with the will, why would Miss Niffin want to kill her already generous employer and benefactor, why indeed?

"As both women alas are gone, we'll never know the truth for sure, but we can conjecture the significance of the raised voices, the argument, if you will, as it now takes on a different color. It appears Miss Niffin wanted, indeed was demanding, more recognition – the money, generous as it might have been, was simply not enough. Miss Wembley in turn was doing her best to remain patient and placate her all too ambitious partner, in the process reminding her she'd been generous and such and Miss Niffin accordingly should be grateful and not make such a scene, or something to that effect.

"And it's here we get to the real motive. You see, Miss Niffin wanted to become the new, publicly acknowledged queen of mystery writers, and in her mind the only way to achieve this was to eliminate Miss Wembley. Thus a certain cruel irony in that the dubious vehicle to bring about this state of affairs was the notion of the proverbial perfect murder. It was almost as though she had borrowed the idea from one of her mistress's stories, or to be more exact, one of *her* stories. Yes, Miss Niffin was the ghost writer for Miss Wembley's best selling mysteries, and we have a multitude of details that reveal this. First – and here we have to go back in time somewhat – the fact that Miss Niffin wrote her thesis on Mary Roberts Rinehart, America's original doyen of mystery writers, thus she knew the genre backwards and forwards. Which underscores an especially bitter turnabout, which I've just hinted at: she may well have gotten the idea from a literary device, specifically the mystery story in which the double stands in for the real murderer. Alas, as Miss Niffin found out, the practice ultimately works no better in real life than it does in fiction.

"There were other clues: Miss Wembley's inability to answer satisfactorily her editor's questions about the content of her novels. And Mr. Doveless breaking off his lessons after only a few sessions when he realized she didn't have the slightest idea how to write a mystery novel, much less teach the art. Even more revealing, another little matter that just couldn't be coincidence, was that her career started to take off right after she met Miss Niffin. There was also evidence that Miss Wembley would not hesitate to steal outright another author's work if it was convenient to do so. Thus in the process she has a little bonus and takes some of the creative pressure off Miss Niffin.

Then there was the outline of a novel and the contents of Miss Niffin's diary found in her hotel room by the ever resourceful Mr. Caballero, all written in an impressionistic, poetic style so reminiscent of the writing style in Miss Wembley's books. Now it becomes blazingly clear what was meant by this cryptic passage from the diary, the over-wrought prose which almost hints at the events to follow : *is there any mystery left in* me ... *do I possess a me, or is it the circumspect nature of things that has brought me to this state.*

"And, most revealing of all, the one thousand dollars per month paid without fail to her bank account in Los Angeles. Blackmail, or perhaps reward? It doesn't matter really; they were a great, but only half attributed, writing team, Miss Wembley, the public face, who played the role perfectly, and Miss Niffin, the unrecognized, all too silent partner. Drudging in the background all these years, desiring public acknowledgment for her role, she finally reached the breaking point where she decided to take matters into her own hands. Really, Mr. Tumworth, I'm disappointed you didn't figure it out long ago."

Mr. Tumworth breathed a long sigh and opened his palms in apologetic fashion, while Miss Lavish listened attentively, implying these details were unknown to her.

Miss Francis continued, "In Miss Niffin's twisted logic, it was a risk worth taking. If her plan succeeded she could begin writing mysteries under her own name. And by way of explanation for her newfound writing skills, she could simply say that, being so close to the great lady for so many years, that some of her magic had rubbed off on her and so on.

"As for the much-referenced will, Miss Niffin probably knew nothing of the contents of either the old will or the new will, perhaps didn't care. This is why I am justified in saying hers was ultimately a crime of passion, not profit, though profit may have eventually flowed as a result. Her plan might have worked, but she made a major, indeed fatal mistake – to engage as her accomplice someone even more ruthless and far more experienced in the real criminal world than she. Exactly how much the actress Miss Leah Lavish knew of Miss Niffin's true intentions and motives, we do not know. Perhaps she will reveal this missing piece to the puzzle in due time."

"You'll get no explanation from me," said Miss Lavish, in flat Midwestern tones, abandoning any pretense to a New England accent. "And, by the way, yes, I do want to engage Mr. Tumworth if he'll agree to represent me."

Nonplussed, Tumworth merely said, "I'll certainly take it under consideration."

"I consider that a yes."

Despite his lukewarm response, Miss Francis was certain he would accept the case. He couldn't resist the publicity, or perhaps the challenge, a trial being held in a foreign country, sensational murder and such. How could he turn it down?

"Captain?" Miss Lavish said, as she offered her hands to be cuffed.

"That won't be necessary," Captain Seguro said in his most suave manner.

Miss Lavish was about to be escorted away by two of his men and she turned and said, "Excellent job, Miss Francis, and yes, I'll say this much: it was put to me by Miss Niffin as a kind of bet between her mistress and Miss Luckigham, one of their practical jokes. She said she'd pay me a thousand dollars for a few hours' work. I never believed her story; the whole thing sounded crazy but I never argue with a paycheck. Actually I thought I would get away with it, my later … improvisation, as you call it. But I underestimated you. My mistake."

She began to walk away, then hesitated, looking back at Miss Francis. "But speaking of wagers, how about a little agreement among gentle ladies? I'd wager that I'll never be convicted, of either crime, either here or in the U.S. I'm confident Mr. Tumworth will take the case and pull something out of his bag of tricks, justifiable homicide, insanity defense, diminished responsibility. What say you, Mr. Tumworth? Or is it just Harrison?"

In his best mock befuddled style, Tumworth offered, "Well, I hardly think …"

"Once again, I'll consider that a yes. But I shouldn't talk so much. My lawyer will disapprove," she said with a conspicuous glance in Mr. Tumworth's direction. "Cheers, Miss Francis. Until we meet again." She then walked out of the room with Captain Seguro's men.

Miss Francis felt what seemed like a cold breeze brush against her back. She was loathe to admit it but she had the terrible suspicion Leah Lavish was right in her prediction that she'd serve no time in prison, and, far worse, they'd meet again some day.

After Captain Seguro's men had whisked Miss Lavish away, Miss Francis perfunctorily wrapped things up, thanking all for their participation and assistance. Looking a little dazed, the principals slowly rose from their chairs and made their way out of the ballroom in ponderous fashion, a couple of them stopping by to congratulate Miss Francis on her fine performance. Even Mr. Tumworth lingered long enough to mumble a few words of praise.

After they all had left Captain Seguro came over to Miss Francis. "In one way Miss Lavish is not alone; I confess I doubted your abilities, too. I was wrong. Let me offer my most sincere congratulations, Miss Francis." He took her hand gently and gave it a discreet kiss. "However, please indulge my curiosity on one matter, if you will."

"I'd be happy to, if I can."

"With so little actual evidence, how did you come to the realization of the identity switch between Miss Lavish and Miss Niffin?"

A faint smile piercing her lips, Miss Francis said, "How does that little French detective put it, something about the grey cells that need to work; in my case they just needed to work a little harder. I confess I was a little slow on the uptake; it seemed I needed the gentle prompting of sleep and rest, even distraction, to put it all together.

"It's now so obvious, even childishly so, right before me. But I just couldn't see it. I just couldn't put all the pieces together, but there they were: someone who looked almost exactly like another person, an obscure actress murdered in mysterious circumstances, all suspects with a perfect alibi. What finally did it was our meeting with that crazy character, our self-confessed murderer. The whole business got under my skin, but I just could quite get a handle on it. Then the dream, a further message about two persons who looked and acted a lot alike and molding into one. But it was when I walked back to the hotel from that comedy of errors with Errol and his pals – "

"I heard about that little interlude. Very colorful."

"Yes, it was, but it was afterward it came to me, when I was walking along the malecón. The murder was done with a double standing in for someone who was here for the conference. After that it didn't take long to realize it had to be Miss Niffin; the other women were too familiar to everybody. From there it was a relatively simple matter to piece together that Miss Lavish had decided to continue the subterfuge, alas with lethal consequences for the unfortunate Miss Niffin, and later, Mr. Thrugg.

"As for the wine glass, well, something about my interview with the supposed Miss Niffin just wasn't quite right: all that hiding her face, the teensy voice and evasive manner, so I got the idea to test the wine glass for fingerprints and hope I'd get lucky. A moot point now, its value as evidence notwithstanding. But the glass will provide the conclusive proof Miss Lavish is, well, Miss Lavish. And that, Captain, is my story."

A hint of a smile creeping into his visage, the Captain shook his head back and forth in a bemused manner, took off his cap, bowed gallantly and said, "An exceptional bit of work, Miss Francis. Again, I most humbly congratulate you on your success." Then he put his cap back on and walked away.

CHAPTER 11

Miss Francis wanted to extend the holiday a few days and the studio was most accommodating. As she lay on Olas Altas Beach enjoying the warm afternoon sun, she could finally relax. She was sweaty and tan and sluggish, and didn't care who knew it. She luxuriated on the near deserted beach in her last few days of freedom, but thoughts insinuated their way into her psyche, musings on the realities of returning to the through-the-looking-glass world of being a movie star.

She reflected on how she never wanted to be a star, how she loathed being a star actually, being gawked at when having lunch with friends and mobbed when going out to have her hair done. Much too much sadness to it, and much too much strain, too much of everything really, which translated into far too little privacy and not enough of lasting value in one's life. But there were rewards and consolations too: a life of plenty, lots of money present and future, not only for herself but as a vehicle to be generous to a worthy charity or needy friend. And more subtle rewards like the opportunity to visit places like Mazatlán and revel in its unmatched atmosphere and mystique. There were more dubious benefits as well, among them her growing repute as an amateur detective.

But, for the moment, that was all behind her; the writerly principals had gone away, along with Johnny Caballero. Even Captain Seguro was being respectful and hadn't shown up for a few days. As for Miss Lavish, she was securely behind bars, awaiting her trial and being looked after by the best attorney money can buy, Mr. Tumworth himself, who had agreed to represent her. There was also the bizarre rumor that Miss Lavish was at work on a book about her most deadly adventure, and that, of all people, Jack Favell and Catherine Wentworth were assisting her on the manuscript. Miss Francis only smiled and gently shook her head in sardonic approval. Birds of a feather, she mused rather uncharitably.

She lounged a bit more on the beach, being careful not to linger too long as she tended to burn in the sun. Then she came back to the front porch and sat in one of the hotel's famous wooden rocking chairs and indulged herself in one of Mazatlán's incredible sunsets. She even started a new book, Agatha Christie's *Murder in Mesopotamia*. She took a break from the book to stare out at the ocean. The sun was setting slowly and the surface of the water reflected its deep burnished redness in smooth splotches toward the horizon. The salt air smelled clean and fresh, a welcome contrast to the dead, charred burned air that hovered in the California desert. She began to walk back to her suite and crossed the tiled lobby. As per usual she stopped by the front desk and asked if there were any messages. One had just come in, from Hollywood.

Dearest Kay,
Word of your activities as a sleuth has gotten around. The legal department over at MGM just contacted me about hiring you to look into a sticky situation. They promise to pay well. Seems one of their starlets has disappeared. All efforts to find her have been unsuccessful. Not releasing a name. Very hush-hush. Let me know your decision. Johnny.

She scribbled some writing on the hotel stationery which was on the counter and gave it to the desk attendant. "Please send this out right away, and have a bellhop come up to my room in twenty minutes, for my luggage. I'm checking out of the hotel."

The attendant asked a concerned, "Miss Francis feeling ok?"

"Miss Francis is very much ok." She began to walk toward the stairs but stopped and turned around. "And don't be so gloomy; remember what the man said, if you can forget yesterday and live only in today, tomorrow can't be too bad." She then walked away.

The man attempted a smile, only half understanding what she had said. Then he looked at the contents of her note.

Dear Señor Caballero,
Regrets to say Miss Francis checked out of hotel one hour ago. Plan to continue holiday. Did not leave forwarding address.
Regards,
Hotel Belmar,
Mazatlán

ABOUT THE AUTHOR

B. C. Stone is the author of *Coda in Black*. He lives in Albuquerque, New Mexico. Before writing novels he worked as a librarian at the University of New Mexico. His maintains a blog on books and writing, *The Vagrant Mood* http://vagrantmoodwp.wordpress.com/

Made in the USA
Charleston, SC
14 February 2013